DEFIANCE

SUBMISSION BOOK THREE

JASON COLLINS

ACKNOWLEDGMENTS

A very special thank you to:

My cover designer, Cate Ashwood Designs.

My editor, Eliza Hunter.

My proofreaders, Leonie Duncan and Shelley Chastagner.

Cover photographer Michael Stokes.

CONTENTS

1

CONNOR

I AWOKE TO THE SOFT RUSH OF AN ARCTIC BREEZE AS IT RIPPLED ACROSS the window, a sort of low whistling that sounded as though it could have come straight from a white noise machine. I lay there in the darkness for a moment, not wanting to open my eyes just yet, even to face the stunning Skyline Lodge that would greet me. I was so comfortable, like I was sleeping in a cloud. It was hard not to just turn over and dive back into a dream. It had been so long since I'd given myself the breathing room to sleep in.

My days were long, hectic, and so swamped in statuesque fitness models that even I felt a little insecure now and then. This week-long photoshoot with some of the finest models our sponsors could trust me with was no exception, luxurious as it was. But to be fair, I sought out the fast-paced life. I loved my work and the lifestyle that went along with it, but there were sacrifices. Cozy, lazy mornings in a fascinating new environment filled with sparkling new experiences and memories to be made was not usually a luxury within my reach.

So naturally, I wanted to make the most of this one.

I sighed and stretched, my body arching under the warm, thick bedsheets. The winds outside seemed to be howling more intensely than I expected, but in a warm, soft pocket like this, it was hard to pay it any mind. I had no idea what the sheets were made of, but I made a mental note to find out, so I could purchase some for my own home. Waking up cocooned in this level of extreme luxury was something I didn't often get to experience. I was a model manager, and too often I spent all my budgeting on making sure my models were comfortable and taken care of while traveling for shoots, putting myself in a cheaper hotel. It wasn't an act of martyrdom, though. It was just that I wasn't the one getting my picture taken—I needed my beauty sleep substantially less than my models.

But I was realizing slowly that maybe I, too, deserved a little TLC from time to time. Even just to keep my mind sharp and my body ready for the toil of a demanding career. Sure, I'd have rather found that comfort in the strong arms of a muscular lumberjack type, but maybe for now I'd have to settle for exquisitely plush sheets. Beggars couldn't be choosers, after all, and these sheets *were* to die for.

I finally managed to open my eyes and slink out of my soft bed to part the curtains at the window, expecting to see that bright Alaskan sun shining on the craggy mountains in the near distance. Last night, as we'd flown in, I had been captivated by the grandiose scale and the almost Impressionist quality of the landscape. Swatches of cobalt and steel, and lush hunter green, all set against the biggest sky I had ever walked beneath. Seeing those mysterious mountain peaks for the first time was... well, it was exactly what I had been searching for. A great wide expanse of opportunity and total immersion.

I wanted to make this land my home, and as soon as I set eyes on those forested mountains and valleys, the voices of the naysayers back home dissipated into nothing. They told me I was too soft, too city-boy to get by out here in the wild, white beyond. I had something to prove here. I had to show everybody what I was capable of, and that meant handling this tricky, elaborate shooting schedule. I had some of my very best modeling clients with me in Alaska, and to a degree, their careers were in my hands. I had to look out for their best interests. I had reassured everyone that no, Alaska was not always a barren snowy wasteland. It was beautiful and lush and full of color. That was the version of Alaska I expected to see from my window this morning.

But to my confusion, all I could see was pure white stretching out in every direction. I blinked a few times, thinking maybe I wasn't awake yet. Surely some deep-sleep dream was still hanging over me, confusing my eyes, but the white expanse remained. My heart began to sink as it dawned on me that we had gotten snow. A whole damn lot of it. And when I looked a little closer, I could see that it was *still* snowing. Beautiful, picturesque little flurries spinning through the air and coating the world around me with pure whiteness. It was awe-inspiring to behold, but my brain was already starting to panic as I rose up out of my post-sleep fog.

No. This could not be happening. I was not ready to accept the version of reality in front of me just yet. I closed the curtains and took a deep breath, thinking perhaps I'd just imbibed a little too much wine on the flight last night. There had been some major turbulence and I was a little bit type A. Just dealing with my flighty, restless models on the long flight was enough to keep me on my toes without the added stress of inclement weather.

But then again… what else was I here for if not something new? An adventure?

I was used to putting out fires—at least figuratively. In my line of work, there were always meetings to attend, time-sensitive emails to answer, shows and venues to book. That kind of responsibility came naturally to me nowadays. It was partly a craving for something different that had edged me into the decision to come to Alaska. But I had not come here without plans in mind. Of course not. With my job, I needed to constantly be scheduling more shoots, more meetups, shaping opportunities out of thin air in some cases. My models had to work, and they could only work if I did. It was a symbiosis, but sometimes a rather tremulous one.

I took a deep breath and opened the curtains again, and reality set in.

This was no mistake, no trick of the eye. I wasn't looking at some beautiful icy winter wonderland via a postcard. It was real. Right there. In front of my very eyes. White flurries blowing on the fierce winds in an almost diagonal direction. Piling up higher and higher.

The ground was no longer within sight. It was just the whiteness. The blank emptiness that curled around the lodge like a frigid infinity scarf, enveloping us in the cold and wet.

No doubt about it. This was a blizzard.

Shit.

I heard some rustling downstairs and realized some of my colleagues must have woken up. I knew it was time for a little damage control.

It was hard not to think of the week going up in flames. The first thing on my mind was the journalist who was traveling with us, Pete. He worked for Western Fitness Quarterly, the magazine putting together the special issue that this trip was for. They had a lot of money backing it in the form of sponsors and ads. As the head writer for the issue, his word would decide whether this week was a success, and the idea of him writing about this whole elaborate *trip* being a bust because of a freak blizzard… it was too much to deal with.

I hastily threw on some pajama pants and a robe and tried not to think about my career as a model manager evaporating before I rushed downstairs, where I found that only a few models were up, but my pair of photographers were definitely wide awake. They were clustered by the big bay window, murmuring frantically, wearing expressions of pure panic. As soon as they noticed I had come into the room, they all whipped around and began hurling questions at me.

"Connor! Look! Snow!" called an aging smoker's voice belonging to a portly guy with dark-rimmed glasses and a salt-and-pepper beard.

There was a time when he was in front of the camera rather than behind it, back when he was a bodybuilder and fitness model in his own right, but nowadays he preferred the technical side of things. He had an eye for detail, always knowing exactly what to focus on and what to fade out. That made him great at action shots, which were very important for fitness photography and modeling. His name was Chuck, and he was usually much more eloquent than this, but evidently panic had made him a little obtuse. His eyes were huge behind the frames of his glasses.

"Yes, I know. I saw it," I said with a sigh.

His frenzied look did not falter in the slightest.

"Well, what do we do?" he asked, throwing up his arms.

One of the fitness models perched cross-legged on the nearby sofa, halfway through an interrupted yoga session no doubt, piped up, looking nervous.

"Is the shoot ruined?" he asked in a faint Finnish accent, tucking a lock of straight blond hair behind his ear.

He was probably my most hippy-dippy model, always doing spreads for fitness magazines and high-art design.

"No, Niko. The shoot is not ruined. Don't freak out. We have to remain calm and work with what we've got," I said in a soothing, professional tone.

"Yes, and what *have* we got?" interjected another model, Paolo.

He was the complete opposite of Niko, with thick Italian features, but then again, models were walking examples of a very specific kind of professionally sculpted look that was ideal for the camera.

"We've got a lot of options, okay?" I assured him, though it was almost more like assuring myself.

I was just trying to put out a few small fires before I tackled the inferno. Vast amounts of money went into these high-end photoshoots, and everything was suddenly on the line. Frankly, I couldn't even fathom how much money we would lose by the hour if we were not able to proceed. Models' fees, photographers, makeup artists, stylists... not to mention the fee for booking the resort itself.

"Oh my god, I'm hyperventilating," murmured one of the photographers, shaking his head as he stared out the window.

His name was David, and he was one of the most talented photographers I had ever met. I loved all my photography friends' work, of course, but David had an eye for lighting and mood that I found impressive. He was a little high-strung, though, as evidenced by the look of pure dread on his face as he looked out the window.

"How the hell is this happening right now?" asked the other model who was downstairs and awake.

His name was Andrew, the lone American of the group. He was

usually more of a surfer than a snowboarder type, but he was hoping to make it work.

I drew a deep breath and slipped right into damage control mode. I held up my hands peacefully and gave them a soft smile. I needed to bring their anxiety level down by about half. Maybe more.

"Calm down, everyone. This is not the end of the world. The shoot is not ruined. We will figure it out. I've got this under control," I assured them.

That was a lie. The truth was that I did not have anything under control. None of us, not even I, were prepared for this. There was not supposed to be a blizzard, according to the planning that went into this trip. Maybe an intern dropped the ball, or maybe the weather really was that unpredictable up here. The ramifications of getting snowed in were starting to weigh on me. Then we heard a loud thump by the front door—the sound of heavy footsteps. My blood ran cold and we all looked around at each other with near-primal fear. This was the kind of lodge that small groups of celebrities might rent out for a private retreat, not a commercial place full of tourists.

"Who could that possibly be?" hissed one of the models, wide-eyed.

The last thing I wanted to admit was that I had no idea. Things were happening so quickly. I had only just woken up and suddenly there was one calamity after the next slamming into me, bam-bam-bam.

But when the door swung open, it wasn't only the gust of icy-cold wind that nearly bowled me right over. It was the enormous, hulking silhouette of a man in the doorway, his arms so thick and muscular that my breath caught in my throat. I was frozen in a split-second of shock, strung up somewhere between panic and intense, undeniable attraction. This man was, to put it lightly, *huge*. And strikingly good-looking on top of it. Even though he was heavily dressed to combat the harsh weather, I could still follow the impressive shape of his body underneath it all. I found myself totally entranced, staring at this absolute mountain of a man who had just appeared at our door in the middle of what looked to be a bonafide Alaskan blizzard. There was a serious, determined look on his angular features. His sensual lips were set in a hard line, his dark brows furrowed. I could see a sharp, hawk like focus and intellect in those piercing eyes, and I knew instantly that this was not a man to be messed with.

On the other hand, he looked like exactly the kind of guy I would let make a mess of me. I could so effortlessly slip into fantasy, imagining the way this hulk of a man could sweep me up off my feet and pin me down wherever he wanted to. I felt a deep twinge of desire at the thought of his huge, calloused hands roving up and down my body, groping and caressing me. That thick, muscular thigh wedging between my legs so we could rut against each other like wild animals desperate for release.

I wanted his sensuous lips to press against mine, softly at first and then with more passion and insistence as our bodies began to mold together. We could rock together in perfect tandem, ratcheting higher and higher like one well-oiled machine until the sacred release. A shiver of pure desire rolled down my spine but I tried my best to hold my head high and look hard. Especially because I didn't recognize the intruder's face at first.

But as he gave us all a curt nod and began unwrapping the layers of scarves, gloves, coats, hats, and boots to reveal more of the ridiculously sexy man underneath, he started to look more familiar. He shut the door behind him, and we all relaxed a little now that the arctic wind wasn't blowing through the living room. We all ogled the man with intrigue, which he promptly noticed.

"You all look like you've seen a ghost or something," he said warily. "Just a little snow."

"A little?" spluttered David.

The handsome guy smiled softly. "That's why you need people like me."

"Oh! Pilot! You're the pilot," Niko burst out, pointing at him.

Of course. My shoulders relaxed a little now that we were all totally sure who this man was. It occurred to me that I had been so wrapped up in my thoughts during the flight—not to mention, drinking wine—to have paid attention to who the pilot was. Even now, I was so focused on admiring his killer physique that I didn't immediately realize he was addressing me.

"So? What is it?" he prompted, hands on his hips.

I blushed instantly, feeling my ears get hot.

"What is what?" I asked nonsensically.

He arched one perfect, thick eyebrow. "Your plan for making this all work once you're snowed in, because let me tell you, that's exactly what's happening," he growled.

My stomach twisted into knots. But I retained my professional demeanor. I had to. My whole team of creatives were relying on me to make sure they produced the career-affirming content we flew all the way out here to get. I needed to stay on my toes and yet also keep my feet planted firmly on the ground. I needed to be daring, but cautious. Innovative, but realistic. That was my role to play in the big production that was working in the modeling industry. Measuring risks, deciding which pains in the ass were worth it and which weren't.

Looking at this gorgeous, rugged pilot in front of me, I made the silent decision not to give up. I had a feeling this guy never gave up on anything. Ever. So maybe I would just view him as my ideal, my example. I rolled my shoulders back and straightened out my posture, clearing my throat.

"I'm the project manager for this shoot," I declared. "I have things under control."

The pilot grinned. "Well, I don't know if it's different where you come from, but out here in the frontier, there's no use fighting the weather. All you can do is be prepared and be cautious."

"I intend to do that," I insisted, a little hint of my stubbornness showing.

But he seemed to find it rather amusing. "You're going to need my help battening down the hatches and taking stock of what resources you have at your disposal here," he said. "Are you willing to take orders?"

I swallowed hard, the pit of desire burning within me growing more intense.

God, he was sexy. A take-charge kind of guy. My type.

But the truth of the matter was he was still a man we barely knew. Was it foolish to place our lives and livelihood in his hands?

"From a man whose name I don't even know?" I asked, but my tone posed it as more of a question than a challenge.

I tried to deny the curiosity fluttering in my chest over what kind of man he was, under all that clothing and muscle. Okay, maybe the muscle could stay—but damn, it made it hard to keep my head clear. And to my surprise, he cracked a smile.

"Out here," he said with an ominous smile. "You might just have to. You're in my neck of the woods now."

A chill sent goosebumps up my neck.

2

GRAYSON

CONNOR TOOK A DEEP BREATH AND RAN HIS HANDS THROUGH HIS HAIR before the flicker of anxiety vanished, replaced again by a confident, professional smile. To anyone else, he looked calm and collected, as if he had been ready for this from the start. I sensed I was the only one in the room who could see right through it.

He was a fish out of water, and I felt like a hungry bear waiting at the riverbanks.

"Well," he said at last, extending a hand. "My name is Connor, so we can start there."

"I know," I said as my bigger hand almost swallowed his in a firm grip I pumped twice. "We've talked once over email."

He looked surprised by that and blinked a few times, glancing back at one of the photographers who shrugged before looking back to my vaguely amused face.

"You mean... *you're* Mr. Cartwright?" he asked slowly. "As in, CEO of Northern Lights Aviation?"

"Northern Lights *Private* Aviation," I corrected him, "but as for me, just Grayson."

"Just Grayson," Connor said with a smile.

He tried to pull his hand away to break the handshake, but I held it in place, staring at him. The blush that splashed across his cheeks was very interesting indeed.

"You didn't answer my question," I said.

"Right," he said at last, looking me up and down one more time. "You make a good... case. Two heads are better than one. Let's put them together. So, you could say you've been in this kind of situation before?" he asked, tilting his head to the side ever so slightly, perfectly serious.

I narrowed my eyes at him and flexed my hands. His eyes flitted to my thick fingers, and the subtle blush in his face was unmistakable. I'd seen it the second we made eye contact and he drank me in with those bright, intense eyes. My face was unreadable, but inside, this little man had my interest.

His body language told me he wanted the same thing I did. The energy crackling between us couldn't just be in my head, whether or not he knew it yet. The urge to get this guy away from the others was burning fiercely, and I meant to make it happen.

"Yeah," my deep voice rumbled. "You could say I have some experience. Sounds like you don't get quite this much snow in California," I added with the faintest shadow of a smug smile.

"No, in LA we just get rush hour traffic that piles up around our houses every now and then," he replied without missing a beat.

I gave a chuckle, then cast a glance around at the other men in the room. Their eyes were on us, and I could see in them a look that was all too familiar to me. The other men in the room were looking to me for leadership.

Or were they looking to both of us?

I might have just seized command of the situation from Connor, but it was clear that the other men respected him. That meant he was good at his job, and in turn, I could respect that from a guy who was by all rights my subordinate now, as far as I was concerned.

And I could work with a respectable man—especially one with a pair of lips like his.

"Sorry," said one of the models I thought I'd heard called Niko. "I'm confused, are we panicking or not panicking?"

"We're good, Niko," Connor said before turning back to me, his attention rapt. "Okay, I'm in, let's do what we need to do. What's first?"

"We need to take stock of the place," I repeated firmly. "And that's what we're going to do. Follow me."

"Anything we should do in the meantime?" one of the photographers asked Connor as I started to walk off.

"Let the others wake up and explain the situation to them if you see them before I do," Connor said as he trotted backward after me, delegating expertly. "Get settled, find some breakfast, and consider this morning a… late start!" he decided before we disappeared from view and headed down the hall.

"This is for the best, honestly," Connor said to me in a lower tone as he followed after. "Full disclosure: I crashed in bed as soon as we arrived last night. I've seen the living room, my suite, and nothing else," he said with a laugh.

"Not an easy trip, if you're not used to it," I said.

"I take that to mean you're used to it?" he asked.

"Have to be," I grunted as the hallway opened up into the large room beyond it. "My living is in the air, and you either learn to rough it or don't stay in the air long. But I'll admit, I don't usually stay in places like this," I added as I raised my eyebrows at what we'd walked into.

Connor stepped further into a large, warm, inviting dining room that spanned the entire width of the lodge, if not most of it. This place felt like it was bigger on the inside than it looked on the outside. It was more like a dining hall—a long table with benches all made of sturdy, rich-smelling wood. Across from the dining table was the large kitchen with all the shelf space a temporary or permanent chef cooking for small groups could ask for. Another wall opened up into one of the lodge's many sitting areas, featuring a large stone hearth and comfortable leather couches around a stylish coffee table. I could almost smell the whiskey that must have been consumed over the years in front of that fireplace.

But cozy as it was, Connor was the most attractive feature by a long shot. I had barely been able to tear my eyes off him while we made our way through the place. The hunger that had hit me at the sight of him reminded me just how long it had been since I'd met someone that I wanted.

And I got what I wanted.

Overhead was an exposed walkway with masterfully worked wooden railings connecting two sides of the guest suites. And on the far end of the space was a full-length window that would let the sunlight in beautifully, if it weren't about to get filled to the brim with snow, depending on how much came down today.

"Unbelievable," Connor said, smiling fondly at everything and taking the scenery in while I took the time to let my eyes flit over his body. "It's one thing to see all this in the pictures the agents sent us, but none of them did it justice."

"This place," I said, walking slowly over to the dining table and resting a hand on the cool surface, "is one of the state's best-kept secrets. You won't find many places like the Skyline Lodge."

"What, do you come here often?" he said with a playful smile, and my heart thudded at the joke.

"Not personally," I admitted, wandering toward the large window. "But private charter airlines up here talk to each other, and we know this is the kind of place celebrities usually come for retreats, that kind of thing. And those celebrities have to get here somehow because nothing bigger than the plane we came in is landing down the mountain in Cornerstone, that's for damn sure."

"When you put it that way, it sounds so remote it really is a secret," he said, raising his eyebrows.

"Coziest secret you'll find around Denali, too," I said. "I hear every piece of material that went into building it is local wood and stone, and every craftsman who worked on it is Alaskan born and bred."

"Really? That isn't in my files, but that's incredible," he said.

"Nothing else could hold up for long on the face of this mountain," I said in a chuckle as I watched the whiteness flying by outside. "You'll get a taste of that soon enough. Come on, let's see if this place is stocked with enough food."

I walked through a door past the kitchen into the food storage rooms, and a light illuminated the whole place with a warm ambiance that felt more at home in some luxury grocery store in the city instead of a storeroom in a lodge. The things we did to make tourists happy were over the top sometimes, if you asked me.

"Oh, yes, this is perfect," Connor said, following me into the room and grinning ear to ear as he perused the shelves.

They were fully stocked with canned and dry goods of the highest quality—the kind that came from specialty stores rather than the usual, basic grocery stores I liked. It was standard practice for any place like this to be fully equipped to keep the occupants alive in a situation like this, but the Skyline could make survival feel like a five-star experience, apparently.

Connor didn't know how good he had it.

"And I see a freezer in the back, there," I said.

Connor immediately hurried to it to pull it open.

He took a deep breath and let his shoulders visibly relax before turning around with a hand over his heart.

"We're going to eat *very* well," he said with a solemn nod and less-than-solemn smile.

"Your company set you up nice and comfortable," I agreed, crossing my arms in the doorway, unconsciously blocking the exit.

I was taking account of everything I saw, but it was hard to tear my eyes away from Connor, especially when that taut, round ass was tempting me so shamelessly in the outline of his clothes. In all the busy chaos of getting this flight together and flying Connor and his crew up here, my co-pilot Landon and I had barely gotten a chance to chat with them. We hadn't necessarily needed to. Our only job had been to fly the crew and all their equipment up to the lodge, spend the night, and fly back, but plans changed on a dime in this part of the world.

I liked men. I always had, and I knew that all too well. I had grown up in a small town where the choices for a love life hadn't been the most abundant, so my track record had been nothing but women until I started the company with the others back in Anchorage. And after that… well, my sister Heather liked to say I was married to my plane.

Connor was my type. Blond, clean cut, clearly in shape, took care of himself, with eyes I wanted to get lost in, and a sleepy, comfortable kind of beauty that came with just waking up within the hour. It was all more than adorable, it was tempting.

And the snow slowly burying us in here was giving me ideas that I was all too suspicious Connor would be down for. But this wasn't just some guy I met at a bar, this was a man who was supposedly organizing this entire trip and managing it personally. He was worth testing.

"I bet some of the models or the photographers know how to cook. Maybe Diego. There was supposed to be a skeleton staff coming, but I assume that's impossible thanks to the snowbanks," Connor said thoughtfully, tapping his chin. "I know, I'll check in with them and write up a rotating schedule to spread out the work evenly among everyone. And if they're willing, we could—"

"We'll cook," I said with such a sudden finality that he looked taken aback and paused. "Don't hold your breath for the staff. Won't be necessary."

"Um…" he said, blinking. "Wait, 'we'?"

I smiled and held up two fingers.

"Two pilots flew you up here, remember?" I said. "The other's my co-pilot, Landon."

"Oh," he said, and I couldn't mistake the brief look of worry in his eyes.

"He's also my cousin," I added. "Hired him a few months ago when he got his license."

"*Oh,*" he said again in a very different tone, relief visibly washing over his face.

I could have pretended not to notice, but Connor was trapped with me—keeping my distance was already out the window. I raised a single eyebrow subtly, and he quickly cleared his throat and gestured to ask me to move aside as he headed for the doorway. He was trying to hide the blush from his cheeks.

"Anyway, shall we?" he said, grinning sheepishly, but I didn't move at first.

I regarded him thoughtfully, taking just enough time to let him see that he had my attention before I nodded and led him out.

"We'll keep it good and filling," I said confidently. "We know our way around a kitchen, believe it or not. It'll keep things simple. Better that way."

"But if—" he started, but he caught himself, and he swallowed. "Well, true, suppose you can't argue with that logic."

The first floor of the sprawling lodge was staggering. On our tour, we passed through no less than three separate sitting rooms, all of them with stunning views from different sides of the lodge, one featuring a fully stocked bar, all of them as comfortable as the one attached to the dining room in their own unique way. This place wasn't just a commercially designed lodge for tourists, that part had been no exaggeration.

We passed the doors to one of the lodge's crowning features, and ironically one we didn't need to worry about for the time being: the world-class gymnasium. This was the kind of facility that could attract a troupe of fitness models, I assumed. I never bothered with fancy gym equipment, but I could respect the precision that went into really rigorous exercise like that. The models might have been odd, but they were in shape, even if they lacked that spark that Connor exuded in every step.

There was a fully functioning sauna not far from the eastern sitting room, and when Connor stuck his head in, I noticed him swipe his tongue across his lips and sensed him almost visibly fight the urge to glance back at me.

"I have to say," he said as he quickly moved on, heading up the stairs toward the lodge's second floor, where the suites were located. "It's nice to see a CEO who takes such a hands-on approach to his business. Back home in LA, you wouldn't find many business executives rolling up their sleeves alongside their peers. You must love your business."

"If you want something done right, you do it yourself," I said simply. "And I have high standards."

"I hear that," Connor said with a smile, seeming to relax a little as we shifted the conversation to talking shop. "I swear, I make schedule spreadsheets in my sleep sometimes. Some of the people back at the office at home joke that my tablet has more timetables synchronized than a clock."

"Our pilots handle themselves, for the most part," I grunted. "We're good at what we do, and we don't need our hands held. Simple."

"I wish I could run a business like that," he said, stepping into the common sitting area on the second floor that branched off into different directions. "The kinds of people I work with have to be handled at just about every step of the job, sometimes."

"What about you?" I asked, turning to him with a challenging smile. "Do you have a handler?"

He was lost for words for a moment, again. I felt like I was going to get a lot of mileage out of this, and I enjoyed that. He moved his mouth silently for a few moments before blushing and giving a nervous laugh.

"No, I suppose I don't, now that I think about it," he said. "I'm usually working my expertise solo. Comes with the territory."

"Then it's your lucky day," I said, stomping past him to lead him down one of the halls I picked at random. "Because you're in my territory now. Consider yourself handled. You're better off."

I could feel him staring at my back—probably a little surprised by my boldness, but I thought it was better not to beat around the bush. If Landon and I hadn't stayed the night, this party might have been a lot more sour.

"Am I, now?" he said, not hiding the hint of a laugh in his voice as he followed.

"You haven't complained so far," I said with a wink, and I felt fire in my heart when I turned my gaze from him.

This was too much fun.

We passed a set of stairs leading up to one of the stone gazebos perched on the "turrets" of the lodge and found our way to a little cafe that seemed tailor made for cozy breakfasts and good coffee—something I had a special love for. The decor up here was as woody and natural-smelling as the first floor's, but it managed an air of comfort that was very rare in my world.

The cafe had another one of those wall-scale windows that the architects seemed to like so much, and I couldn't blame them. The cafe overlooked the gymnasium, where all the gleaming equipment and pristine mirrors stood proudly waiting for use below. Two of the other hallways that branched off from the common area led to the two wings where all of us were staying in five-star quality suites, each one a self-contained vacation in its own right, in my opinion. Then again, Landon and I both liked to keep to ourselves.

The last room we explored was at the far end of the VIP wing where Connor was presumably staying. It was a lounge, but it featured a large wine rack and decor made to look like an old-fashioned drawing room, complete with a pool table, generous seating to sip wine at, and large, luxurious Persian rugs on the floor.

"So," I said as Connor drifted toward the wine rack curiously. "We have a fully stocked kitchen, the fact that power's still on tells me there's an efficient generator system keeping things running, and there's so much room to spread out that some of you probably wouldn't even see each other all day if you wanted some peace and quiet."

"Maybe I had a knee-jerk overreaction to that aspect of this morning," he admitted as he scratched the back of his neck, reading a wine label. "Plus, that does make it easier to ignore the fact that I still need a plan to figure out what we're going to do this week. There's a lot of money backing this trip, if that isn't obvious. It was supposed to be this gorgeous outdoor series of shots of all these acclaimed fitness models that are—seriously—some of the cream of the crop," he said in that increasingly enthusiastic tone of someone talking about his passion. "But I don't have to tell you we're out of our element again. There are so many factors flying around that I can't keep up."

"You're overwhelmed," I pointed out as I approached him slowly from behind. "Stressed. This is a hell of a lot for one man to shoulder, much less be held responsible for."

"That's another thing," Connor said, setting the wine bottle back and shaking his head. "Pete Russo, the journalist flying with us—he's supposed to do an article covering all this. He told us flat out he'd stay in his room for most of the time, so he only gets to see the parts of this trip that'll look best on paper, you know? And I'm starting to worry with the snow piling up, he… might be in his room longer than he expects," he finished, wincing.

I was so close to him I could reach out and touch him. So I did. One thick arm reached out and rested on his shoulder, and when he turned his head, I held his chin and gently made him look up at me. His face went cherry-red, and his mouth fell open.

"Grayson…?" he asked softly, stunned but not unhappy.

"You're trying to bite off more than you can chew," I growled, moving closer and looming over him. "All you're going to do is burn yourself out. I have experience managing people. And I'm going to steer us through, however long this lasts. But to do that… you need to give up some control," I added in a hungry tone.

"What are you—" he said, but he trailed off as my nostrils flared and I took in the scent of yesterday's cologne still on him, mixed with his natural scent that was driving me wild.

"And if you want to give up *complete* control," I said in a dark, ominous growl, "you're going to meet me in the sauna downstairs after the hearty dinner I'm going to feed you. Do you understand what I'm telling you?" I asked, narrowing my eyes.

Connor looked like he was peering up at me and into a dream come to life—the same way I was looking down at him. There was no mistaking the tension between us anymore. That made Connor squirm, and I loved it.

He gave a single, soft nod of his head.

"Good," I said, letting go of his chin. "Now, I'm going to check the nuts and bolts of this place. See you at dinner," I added, turning my back to him and stomping out of the room, feeling a smile spread across my face knowing that I'd just left Connor thunderstruck.

This might have been the one blizzard I was grateful for.

3

CONNOR

Surely I must have been losing my mind. All throughout the day, I had been walking around in a daze, my eyes idly taking in my surroundings while my inner imagination sculpted a new world out of fantasies which hung over my head like a hazy veil. I was usually the guy with the razor-sharp focus, the ability to withstand any conditions in the pursuit of my career. I put my job first, always. It was the way things had always been, for as long as I could remember.

In my family, success was hardwired into our brains. My parents were tireless workers, endlessly hustling to keep good food on the table and a sturdy roof over our heads. I learned early on that if you could find a job that both paid the bills and nourished your spirit, there was nothing greater you could achieve in life. Well, except for maybe love. That was another thing I had learned from my parents—what a good, strong relationship built on trust and mutual respect could look like, how smoothly they could run like a machine. Two pieces, swinging back and forth to keep every little star and spangle of life in order. It was all about climbing the ladder together, filling their world with shiny things and new experiences. Growing up, there were definitely some moments in which I felt my parents were trying to keep up with the Joneses, as they say, but in their defense, they kept up pretty damn well. Maybe it was the way they made a perfect team, keeping a united front even when they disagreed on something. They constantly built each other up, and they did the same with me.

That was probably how I ended up like this: successful, artistically-fulfilled, but undeniably, unavoidably alone. Not completely, of course. I was relatively close to my family, and I had plenty of friends in the industry: photographers, models, camera techies, studio curators, gallery owners alike. There were tons of people I could call to help me in a pinch. There were tons of people I could meet up with for coffee or a beer to chat about work and reminisce about art history together. Hell, there were even people I could have called to come stay the night with me if I wanted. I knew I was well-liked, well-regarded in my usual social and professional circles.

But the truth was that I didn't have time. Rather, I didn't *make* time. Not for something so lofty and intangible as love. Sex, maybe. I thought about it sometimes. But there was a part of me deep within my soul that knew I didn't want just that. Just sex? No falling in love? No future? No dreaming and scheming about the golden years? I didn't want someone I didn't know. I wanted someone whose soul could recognize mine. I wanted that sweeping fairytale scene, that bright and shining ideal.

But that wasn't reality. And for someone who was normally such a realist, I had to admit I was a little naive in the ways of love. In my career, people looked to me to be a problem solver. Connor, king of getting shit done. Colleagues asked me for advice. Models recommended me to their aspiring model friends. Photographers clamored to work with me on-set. Because I wasn't just the guy who wrangled the models, I was their manager. Their friend. Their confidante. Occasionally a deliverer of tough love conversations. I knew how to keep people calm and happy and in the know. I was good at making connections everywhere I went.

People saw me as cool and put-together. Which was why I couldn't figure out how my encounter with that handsome pilot earlier today had me so riled up. I had dealt with more intimidating men, more nerve-wracking circumstances than this. I was a pretty competent guy, overall. But something about that man, with his piercing eyes and that jet-black hair, that body of sinewy, flexing muscle... it had me intrigued. You would think by now I might be immune to the intoxicating effects of good-looking men. After all, I did spend a substantial chunk of my waking hours surrounded by professional male models. Men with jawlines that could cut glass. White teeth that would glow in a dark room. Flawless skin and never an ounce of unnecessary body fat.

But Grayson was not like that. He was different. He was real. Not to say that my models were fake, but there was a sort of curated look to them. They wore the right brands, they cuffed their jeans the right way, they tucked in the fronts of their shirts the same way, in line with current fashion trends. Looking at one of my models on a set was a little bit like watching a human being embody a brand or a commodity. Every angle, every inch of innovation had to be examined and labeled marketable. What wouldn't sell didn't print. And whoever was wearing it didn't land roles. Buddying up with brands and sponsors, molding one's public and sometimes even private persona to fit a prescribed market model, it was all par for the course. Everyone was hyper-conscious of who they were, who knew their name, who would recognize them in a crowd. On display at all times.

Grayson, however, was the opposite. He didn't seem to play by anybody's rules besides his own. He was completely and utterly in control of himself and his destiny. He was a grizzly bear of a man with a quiet restraint that elevated him far above the beast. He fascinated me. He caught like a hook in my imagination, all my little scattered fantasies gathering in to cluster around the image of Grayson in my mind.

The intensity of his gaze, the penetration of his eyes into my very soul. The soft pull of a passing smile at the corners of his sensuous lips. It disappeared just as abruptly as it arrived, leaving me instantly wistful and pining for it to come back. I wanted to see him smile, to hear that low growl of a laugh that gave me goosebumps and made my heart race faster. I longed to feel his hot breath on my neck, the ticklish pleasure of his lips whispering a soft line of filthy, delicious words into my ear. I wanted to take those huge, powerful hands and guide them to my waist, my hips, my ass. He could pin both of my wrists so easily with one hand, his other hand free to wander down between us. Maybe he would stroke himself as he rocked against me, grunting his pleasure with every thump-thump against the wall or the kitchen counter or wherever the hell he wanted me. Or maybe he would slide those calloused fingers up and down the length of my cock, caressing the swollen pink head while his own shaft pressed long and hard against my thigh…

Damn it. I looked down at the front of my dress pants. They were perfectly, expertly tailored to suit my body, but right now even my tailor's skills could not have accommodated the wardrobe malfunction I was having. My cock was twitching and thickening up, itching for me to touch it, to give myself the release of pent-up tension I so desperately needed. It was frustrating; I was normally so good at controlling myself and clamping down on my desires in order to get the job done. Work usually filled all the physical energy and mental space I had, leaving no room for fantasy and therefore, pesky erections at inopportune times.

"Barely know the guy and this is how he affects me," I sighed to myself, looking in the mirror at the bulge in my pants.

I untucked my dress shirt and let it hang while I waited for the arousal to pass. It was a little painful, my need was so intense, but I refused to give in to my bodily urges. It was just a craving. Just a little crush. Nothing to worry about. I briefly considered just taking a few minutes to bang out a quickie, just to get it over with. But what if that only solidified my feelings for the guy? What if indulging in my steamy fantasy would somehow cross the wires in my brain that would make me catch true, authentic feelings for this man who was clearly way out of my league.

"Ugh," I groaned, realizing with mingled disappointment and relief that my anxiety over how to deal with my feelings for Grayson had successfully sated my sex drive for the moment.

Thank god, too. I had a nice dinner downstairs with the cast and crew and—gulp—the pilots to look forward to. I needed to work out all my weirdness about Grayson now before heading downstairs, otherwise I might get so butterfly-stomached and tongue-tied that I would make a fool of myself. I needed the full trust and respect of my team if we were going to have any shot of making this situation work. I needed to keep morale high. So I tucked away my fantasies for a later date, finished getting dressed for dinner, took a deep breath, and stepped out into the hallway to go downstairs. Of course, within seconds of stepping out of my doorway, I nearly bumped smack dab into someone larger than me who was coming from the opposite direction. I fell back a few steps, blinking in confusion and trying to regain my composure.

"I beg your pardon—" I began reflexively, until I noticed that the man was, in fact, the same guy I had just been fantasizing about.

"My mistake," Grayson said in that low, gritty, almost-drawl.

God, he looked so good. He was dressed to kill, not in trendy clothing, but in the kind of utilitarian comfort style you would expect from a powerfully built Alaskan alpha male. Simple lines, flat colors. Nothing flashy, but then again, you didn't need to add much flash to his appearance to improve it. He was damn near perfect just as he came.

I stared at him, my mouth hanging open as my brain scrambled for literally anything intelligent to say. But I was speechless. I, a person who spent most of my time strategizing and negotiating with others, was at a loss for something to say. Grayson was simply gorgeous, too much to take in all at once. I wished that I could stop time, just for the opportunity to get a closer look at all the glorious angles, curves, and hard lines of his beautiful body. I wanted to commit his face to memory, keep a framed picture of those hawk-like eyes hanging in the forefront of my mind. But instead, all I could do was stare. His mouth briefly upturned into the shape of a smirk, and my heart skipped two beats.

He knew. He could tell I was enraptured. And I was. No denying it.

Grayson leaned in close and murmured in that rasping tone, "Was just coming up here to let you know that dinner's ready."

I nodded slowly, as though my brain was taking the time to savor every word that fell so smoothly from his perfect lips. Finally, the meaning soaked through and I smiled. My cheeks burned like before. Damn my body chemistry for making my emotions so visible.

"Oh. Well, thank you. I was about to make my way down there," I replied.

"Perfect. You hungry?" he asked gruffly.

Butterflies in my stomach again. "Hungry for what?" I murmured, my eyes lingering over those lips, wondering what it would feel like to press mine against them.

"For dinner?" he prompted, raising an eyebrow at me.

I winced slightly, knowing I'd been caught slipping. "Oh, right. Yes. Starving," I said.

"Good. Let's go on down," he said.

Gesturing for me to follow, he sauntered down the hallway to the stairs. I trundled along behind him stiffly, concentrating on not letting my eyes lock onto the swagger of Grayson's gait, the taut roundness of his perfect ass in those trousers. He was a wet dream come to life if I ever knew one, but I had to keep my dirty thoughts to myself. Now was not the time to be ogling one of our new team members, not with the group still under stress over the necessary changes in plan we would have to make.

We entered the large dining area, where the photographers, models, the other pilot, and the journalist were gathered. I took an empty seat next to Grayson at the table and tried my best to keep up the pace with the conversations bouncing back and forth while still not making a fool of myself in front of Grayson. The meal itself was incredible, just platter after platter of the most sumptuous, luxurious dishes I had ever seen. There was a gigantic charcuterie platter of cheeses, smoked salmon, bear meatballs, moose sausage, snap beans, berries, cream cheese, rhubarb jam, and crudités. There was a huge handmade glazed ceramic bowl filled with roasted root vegetables, flavored with tart cranberry, sea salt, and olive oil. Freshly-baked loaves of fragrant, herby bread, slathered with thick pats of real, full-fat butter. Tureens of salty, savory gravy that were perfect for soaking the sliced bread. Bottles of wine poured freely and there were plenty of ice-cold beers to go around. Every plate that passed around the table brought new pleasures and delights, and I found my stomach yowling with hunger, the first and only thing to properly distract me from my other current fixation: Grayson.

Watching him interact with his own colleague versus my people was entertaining, to say the least. He and his pilot friend, Landon, talked so seriously. They used a lot of technical jargon. There were even some inside jokes that gave me a strange twinge in my stomach I didn't quite know what to make of. But then he would try to join in a conversation with my model clients and the gap between life experiences there was… stark.

"Grayson, you remember that time you got stranded out on that snowy plateau awhile back?" piped up Landon, eyes bright.

Grayson nodded and sighed. "Yeah. It was a nightmare, but I pulled through. Luckily, the only thing more stubborn than the Alaskan winter is my will to survive," he said.

"Damn," I murmured.

"What?" he asked, looking at me quizzically.

My face flushed a deeper red and I quickly busied myself with some roasted potatoes as I mumbled back, "Nothing. Just impressive."

"Oh, are we talking about near-death experiences?" joined in one of the models, a wiry pretty boy with taut muscles but an almost soft-looking face.

His name was Erik, and he was the youngest of my clients, barely over twenty years old. He had been a city pool lifeguard as an adolescent to put himself through school, and luckily, he'd earned a scholarship for swimming that kicked off his career. He was in peak physical condition but he was a little less bulky than the others. In fact, his willowy height and build had landed him a couple of editorial fashion features, too. He was a cross-learner, working comfortably in the fitness world and the fashion world at the same time. But he was still a young guy, and sometimes his true age would peek through his professional persona.

"Why, you got one?" scoffed another model, Tomas.

Tomas was a little rougher around the edges, a former MMA

fighter-turned-fitness model who had a flair for the dark and gritty style. He was kind of our resident bad boy, if I were to put him in a box like that.

The guys went on sharing their near-death experiences, and it quickly became clear that there were, in fact, varying degrees of severity in this realm. For Tomas, he was nearly stampeded by a bull on vacation in his home country of Spain. Erik was threatened by a drunken man in a bar bathroom in Berlin. Landon came face to face with a polar bear on a northern excursion. Niko once got severe food poisoning from expired kale. I had almost been hit by a city bus once as a child. But Grayson seemed to have an endless list of near-misses and dangerous risk-taking that only made me more and more intrigued by him.

So when the pilots excused themselves from dinner early and Grayson's eyes lingered for just a moment too long on mine, I was reminded with a jolt of the offer he had made me earlier. My appetite for food disappeared. My desire to keep up with the conversation at the table disappeared. All the noise fell to a shrill ringing in my ears and my heart thumped wildly in my chest. Did I dare take him up on his offer? Was I crossing a line?

Of course. Of course, that was crossing a line. But I was helpless. I had to cross it.

I quietly excused myself. I walked out of the dining area and, taking deep breaths, crossed the property to the sauna. I felt like my heart might just pound right out of my chest as I reached for the doorknob and slowly turned it, my fingers clammy with anxiety. I wanted this. More than anything. But I didn't quite know what to expect. It seemed almost too good to be true. For a moment, I thought about backing out. Washing my hands of the temptation and going upstairs to the privacy of my bedroom to work out my frustration. But when I felt the steam hot against the door, I got a flash in my mind of what Grayson's body might look like inside, all glossy and slick with oil, with sweat. It made my mouth water to think about it.

So I did what I had to do, what my body compelled me to do.

I opened the door.

A burst of humidity came rolling out over me, and through the fog clearing, I saw the rippling, impressive back muscles of the most devilishly attractive man I had ever set eyes on. There was a towel around his waist, but his full upper body in all its glory was on display, rendering me tongue-tied yet again. Grayson looked back at me over his bulky shoulder, a twinkle of mischief in those eyes.

"You showed up," he remarked gruffly, looking me up and down.

I bit my lip and closed the door behind me. "How could I have said no?" I murmured.

"I need to know," he grunted. "Do you really want this?"

My stomach was twisting into knots. Was this really happening?

"Of course. Of course, I do. God, I want this," I confessed.

He smirked. "Good to hear." He stood up and turned around, towering over me.

"But," I hesitated, "don't get me wrong, but… you don't seem like the *type*."

Grayson scoffed and reached down to cup the back of my head possessively, his gaze boring into my soul. "Labels don't mean shit out here. If I like what I see, I jump on it. That's how I like to stay in control. And if you want a taste of that, you'd better start taking those clothes off for me," he commanded.

He let go and I stepped back a little, my heart racing as I slowly began to strip out of my clothes. Grayson never took his eyes off me, not even for a second. He drank in every inch of my body as I exposed it piece by piece. I found that the more naked I got, the more comfortable I began to feel. I was easing into something warm and inviting, yet so exciting that it made my heart gallop. And when he ordered for me to get on my knees, I was all too eager to do as I was told. I dropped down on my knees, peering up at him as he took my chin in his hand. He gazed down into my face, those eyes blazing with want and need. I was going to give him what he needed. I was going to fulfill that desire. My only motivation was to make him feel so good.

He dropped his towel to the floor and I actually gasped at the glorious cock that bounced free. He was huge, every inch of him velvety smooth and hard as marble. I greedily wrapped both hands around its full length, pumping up and down in a slowly increasing rhythm. Then I leaned in and flicked my tongue around the sensitive head, tugging him into my mouth. I heard him groan and one of his arms reached out to steady himself against the wall. Everything was so hot—physically and figuratively. Sweat beaded and rolled down my back. I drank up the delicious masculine scent of his body as I bobbed up and down on his cock, eager to get him off.

"You want to taste me, hmm? You want to top off your Alaskan dinner?" he groaned.

With his fingers twisting in my hair and his cock twitching in my mouth, brushing against the ticklish back of my throat, I continued to suck him off harder and harder, picking up the pace until his hips were pistoning back and forth, pummeling into my mouth and throat. I was nearly gagging, but I didn't care. I was fully focused on my one goal: to make him come.

And when I moaned around his cock in my mouth, sending little vibrations up through his core, I got precisely what I wanted. He seized up and held my head in place as he came, spurting hot spunk down my throat. I lapped it up eagerly, moaning and licking my lips. He rocked gently through the last few drops, then pulled me up and kissed me full on the lips. Sighing, he ran his hand down the side of my face, a fire blazing in his eyes.

"How did I do?" I asked breathlessly.

He smiled, pressing a thumb against my lower lip. "Let's just say you're coming to bed with me tonight," he growled.

4

GRAYSON

How long had it been since I had woken up with someone else in my bed?

I knew I was awake, but I didn't let myself stir just yet. I could feel Connor's body heat at my side, not quite touching me but close enough that we could keep each other warm. He must have rolled to his side in his sleep. A soft smile crossed my lips in the darkness. *Rebellious,* I thought. Even in his sleep, he thought he could get away from me.

Maybe it was a little hasty of me to think about Connor that way so soon. He had drunk from my staff just the once, and I had so cruelly left him aching all night next to me. But had it really been just that? It sure didn't feel like it.

I had fallen asleep last night to the best rest I'd gotten in years, hands down. The fancy mattress that was firm with just enough give probably helped, but the relaxation I felt from head to toe came from within. The satisfaction I had felt when my pearly come surged into his mouth was beyond compare. Just the memory of it made my cock twitch and start to swell.

My chest rose as I drew in the cool air of the still bedroom. The hints of pine and resin in the crisp, frosty air made me feel like I was standing in the middle of the woods outside down in Kenai on a cool autumn day. I could envision the tall, proud trees standing in a sea of mist that made the place look like something out of a fairy tale book just before the story took a dark turn.

Damn, I wanted to turn my nose up at the decadence of this place, but that was impossible. I didn't take vacations often. When I did, I liked the kind that involved a lot of travel, roughing it, and making memories with close friends, like the road trip through Canada I took with the guys a few months ago. I prided myself on being low maintenance and never wanting more than I needed to get by. That kind of attitude suited a pilot's life. But this lodge was warming my heart up to it pretty quickly.

Getting oral from a man in a sauna anywhere earns a place bonus points in my book.

Finally, I turned my head to look at Connor's silhouette in the shadowy room. The sight of him looking so vulnerable was enough to make my blood run hot and stiffen my cock the rest of the way. My body suddenly ached with a pang of desire for him, and I almost wanted to punish him for making me feel such a craving so early in the morning.

There it was again, that dark direction my mind took when I thought about Connor. Domination felt like such a clunky word for my urges in bed, but I was no stranger to it. In fact, I was something of a specialist. I knew what I liked, and I liked getting it, but having it offered up to me by someone like Connor, who was already drop-dead gorgeous? That was poetry in motion.

I decided to wake him. My body clock was precise, so I knew it was time to get up, and I wanted to bring Connor into the day with a little taste of last night, just in case the initial rush had worn off.

One of my thick arms slid under his pillow, and the other wrapped over him and pulled him closer with a low, hungry murmur. Connor woke slowly, pushing against me at first and then stretching out and realizing that he was being held. He murmured pleasantly as my hands felt up his warm, firm muscles.

My lips pressed a kiss to his neck, and the hand over his topside reached down between his legs to grip the thick shaft I felt. My smile grew. He was already stiff with morning wood, and he groaned softly when he felt the firm grip of my hand starting to move up and down the bulging shaft.

"Morning," I growled in a low tone right up against his ear, and I felt him shiver at my very touch.

"Hey," his sleepy, scratchy voice replied as he smiled warmly up at me and turned to face me in bed.

I kept him from turning all the way and instead held his cock upright to keep massaging it. I pushed my hips into his thigh and ground against him as I hugged him closer. The warm skin of our bodies came together in a comfortable, cozy mess of sinful feelings that I chose to wake us up with.

He kept trying to roll over to face me, but I held perfect control of his body. If I didn't want him to turn a certain way, he didn't, and if I wanted to feel his cock twitch at my gentle but relentless grasp, I would feel it. And I did.

He arched his back and squirmed in my grasp as I felt the fire welling up in my body, and frankly, I debated whether or not to act on it. If I went much further, I wouldn't be able to hold myself back. I pushed my hips against Connor's ass and held it, letting him feel the soft, ominous pulse of my shaft as I finally let him turn to face me.

Those eyes were my weakness.

"Surprised you got any sleep, with this bothering you," I growled, and his blushing face split into an embarrassed smile.

"We all have our weaknesses," he teased, letting his eyes close a moment as my thumb teased the tip of his cock. "But I'm glad to see you still here."

"Don't tell me you have that problem often," I said with a chuckle.

"Well, you could say I'm married to the job," he said as he cuddled closer to me. "I was just worried it would be awkward if..."

I tightened my grip on his cock and drew it up just enough to silence him with a sudden hiss of a breath drawn in sharply. I'd sent a ripple of pleasure up his body, and his blush grew all the more.

Deciding to get more possessive, I turned him around so that his ass faced me, and I slid my stiffness between his cheeks so that it pinned my upright cock between my abs and the small of his back. The pressure I felt on the underside of my rod was soft and firm at the same, and at last, I felt like my body had woken up enough to really throw its weight around today.

Too bad fooling around in bed with Connor was too much fun.

"I like you, Connor," I growled, more of a statement of fact than being cute. "I like how you talk, I like how you feel, and I like how you take orders. Man and woman are just words to me. I know what I want when I see it. But not many people know how to give me what I want."

"They're missing out," Connor said, and the way his voice purred those wonderful words soothed my soul like a balm on a fresh burn.

My entire body ached for him, and I had a hard time restraining it. Connor seemed different today, even as he stirred in bed and tried to roll out. All the anxiety and tension I had seen so clearly just under the surface of the man was… maybe not gone, but it had been toned down some. If he had been a thunderstorm inside yesterday, he was a steady shower with distant rumbling in the clouds today.

I didn't want to get my hopes up that my dominating tendencies could be as good for him as they were for me. But it was hard to ignore the evidence, as early as it was.

Connor tried to roll out of bed, but I grabbed him by the hips and pulled him back in with me, chuckling. He broke down laughing softly despite himself, but just as he started to relax once more and let himself sink back into my arms and stroke his cock more, he froze.

"Hold on," he said, sitting up as I let him go.

His eyes were at the drawn curtains, and I saw the gears turning in his head. He hurried out of bed, and I rolled my eyes as I watched him pull his pants on and thrust the curtains open. His jaw dropped, and he put a hand to his mouth.

"Oh my god," he said.

I approached, nude, and I smiled as I set two heavy hands on his shoulders and looked out at the altered landscape outside. Freshly fallen snow blanketed the mountainside so pristinely that it could have been a painting. Snow was still falling steadily, too, but the worst of the storm seemed to have passed. But I could see why Connor was disoriented—the "ground" was now several feet higher than it had been last night.

"It looks like we're on the *first* floor," he said faintly.

"Welcome to your first proper snow-in," I said, squeezing his shoulders. "These are no joke. That right there is a snowbank, and it's a lot more solid than you expect when you think of the light, fluffy stuff."

"Sure, yeah," he said absently, eyes wide, and he broke away to hastily start putting on a clean set of clothes.

I watched him with a raised eyebrow, still naked, cock still at half-mast as I stood in the window like a silent guardian.

"Sure you're not the one having second thoughts about last night?" I asked, not believing it for a second but still wanting to be clear.

"You have no idea how much I needed last night," he assured me, giving me a blushing grin that made my heart pound faster. "Everything yesterday was good—so much better than it would have been if you hadn't been here. But I need to touch base with the others, I-I don't have a solid plan yet, and we need one like, yesterday!"

"Just don't get ahead of yourself," I warned him as he put on his belt, and I approached him to help fix his tie briefly. "One step at a time, one breath at a time."

"Thanks," he said, running his hand through his hair once he had finished dressing.

He glanced at himself in the mirror, then back to me, and the reminder that I was stark naked seemed to give him the momentary snap out of his hyper-focused trance that he needed. He smiled, took a deep breath, and just like that, he was the perfectly confident and composed manager I'd seen when I walked through the door.

"I'll catch up with you," he said, and he darted out of the door.

I smiled as I pulled my own clothes on and stretched, and after a moment's thought, I decided now was as good a time as ever to check in with my own people, since we had the chance. I made my way down the hall to the other wing of the lodge, where Landon's door was already ajar. I rapped on the doorframe.

"You up?" I grunted.

"Yeah," he grunted back.

We were a family of few words.

Landon was already dressed, and he was in the process of getting his laptop hooked up and open on the desk by the room's large window. I chuckled at the place as I entered, noting the way each suite in this lodge seemed to have its own unique character to it.

"Gotta say, this job is going to spoil you," I said as I approached my cousin and pulled up a chair behind him to face the screen. "Getting holed up in this lodge is the best perk I've seen in all my years of flying."

"Better than that bottle of scotch you got from that collector up in the North Pole?" he asked with a gruff smile.

"Mm, forgot about that—make this second best," I corrected myself before nodding to the screen. "Guessing you had the same idea as me."

"Time to give Heather the gory details?" Landon asked. "Yeah. Right after I ask what happened with you last night."

I raised an eyebrow, but Landon was kin—Cartwrights didn't hide many secrets from each other, and soon, we were both giving each other the same gruff, knowing smirk before I shook my head.

"All I'm going to say is, maybe the hype about California isn't all wrong," I said with a soft laugh, and before a grinning Landon could reply, I reached over and touched the screen to start a video call with the hangar back home.

A few moments later, the screen flicked on, and we saw my little sister Heather at the desk, adjusting her screen. She had her hair loosely tied back and a steaming coffee in front of her in my own travel thermos.

"Damnit, I knew I was forgetting something," I said.

"It's the best one, Gray, you know that," Heather said before I'd even finished, and I snorted a laugh.

"Morning," I finally greeted her, and Landon nodded at my side. "How's everyone holding up over there?"

"Daniel just took off for that farm outside Juneau," she said, glancing at the schedule. "And for today, I have 'see how boned Grayson is' on my to-do list, scribbled down after Landon sent me a message about the blizzard," she finished with a plaintive frown at the screen. "What's going on up there, are you two alright?"

"We're safer than we've ever been," I said, barely even joking. "But I wanted to see if you've got eyes on the storm, so we can figure out how long we'll be pinned down up here with Connor."

"Who?" Heather asked.

"The client," I corrected myself, trying not to laugh at the fact that I'd almost forgotten there were men besides Connor at the lodge. "They're up here for some kind of big photoshoot, and since we're piled in with them, I'm going to lend a hand."

"Not like I could stop you even if I was there," Heather said with a laugh. "Alright, I'll see if I can shuffle some of the new hires around. As for this storm, let's see..."

As Heather pulled up her weather feeds and flicked through them, I heard the sound of a footstep outside the door. I didn't have to turn my head to know Connor was eavesdropping. He had probably overheard our conversation and realized that he could get some info to his own benefit. I didn't want to call him out, so I pretended not to notice.

"Looks like the snow shouldn't be coming down too much longer, but this thing surprised everyone, so you never know..." she thought out loud, drumming her fingers on the desk. "I'd say between the snowfall and how long it's gonna take to clear enough to get you back in the air, you'll be grounded for about a week when it's all said and done."

"A week?!" Connor blurted from the doorway, and all three of us looked around to see him standing outside it.

Caught red-handed, Connor stepped inside and cleared his throat. "I was just passing by, and uh... overheard. Hey there."

"Hi!" Heather said with a cheerful wave while Landon and I stared, and I gave a lone nod.

"So, I heard a week," he said, shutting the door behind him. "You don't mean a whole week of being snowed in, do you?"

"Afraid so," I said.

"That's… that's the whole shoot!" Connor said.

"The snow has to stop, then it has to melt enough that we can get out there and start shoveling," I explained in a firm, simple tone. "This isn't Anchorage. You won't have plows clearing the streets ASAP. Out here, you do it yourself."

"We're going to have to fly back at the end of this week, though," Connor said. "The models and photographers and the journalist all have other work to get back to."

I took a deep breath and glanced at my sister on the screen. "Heather, send us an email with the details if you could. I'm going to have a chat with my client."

"Sounds good," Heather said with a laugh. "Stay warm, everyone!"

Landon cut the call and stood up slowly, giving me a nod and stalking out of the room past Connor to give us some privacy. Connor looked at me as if I was about to scold him, but instead, I put a hand on his shoulder and peered down at him seriously.

"Listen," he said. "We're all trapped here in the same lodge this week. You're used to being able to control the situation. You're good at that—I recognize it in you," I added, and a blush crossed his face. "But out here, you can't control the weather, you can just adjust your flight plan, you hear me? They're going to be looking to us to keep it together, because they know we're running the show. You let me steer you in the right direction, and you'll be able to steer *them* in the right direction. Understand?"

Connor was utterly in my control, but even so, he held his head high and nodded after taking a deep breath. "You're right. We can do this. So, going outdoors just isn't happening, right?"

"What we're going to do about that is get creative," I said. "If we can't run up to the mountain peaks, use what we have around us—but one thing at a time. What was the plan for this morning if you weren't snowed in?"

"The models should be hitting the gym for their workout routines right about now," he said. "I already saw a few headed that way. Then an outdoor shoot, which obviously can't happen."

"Workout," I said with a grin. "Good. That gives me an idea. Let's get changed and head downstairs. Now."

5

CONNOR

I SAT ON THE EDGE OF THE BED, WATCHING WITH CLOSE ATTENTION TO the way that Grayson peeled his shirt up off his body and neatly folded it, draping it over the back of a chair. His glorious musculature rippled and flexed in the strange glowing light of a snowy day. I found myself mesmerized by the curve of his waist and the thick barrel muscles of his limbs. The guy had thighs that could crumble brick, and an ass so round and taut it made my mouth water. He was a masterpiece work of art come to life and I could hardly believe what I was looking at. He was beautiful in a wild way, just a tinge of danger to spice up his appearance. I supposed he was rather like the land of Alaska itself: wild and fearfully beautiful. Utterly raw and authentic. Straightforward and yet still somehow full of secrets meant to be discovered.

"You should take a picture," he said suddenly, jolting me from my thoughts.

I blinked rapidly in confusion. "A picture? What? I'm not a photographer," I spluttered.

Grayson smirked and put his hands on his hips, looking amused.

"It was a joke. You know, take a picture, it'll last longer?" he clarified.

I felt my cheeks burn hot and I looked away, shaking my head.

"Oh. Right. Yes, sorry. I didn't realize I was staring," I said hastily.

"It's alright. There's a lot to look at, I suppose," he replied in a gruff but friendly tone.

"You are filling out those workout pants pretty well, I must say," I blurted out before I had a chance to think better of it.

My face felt like it was beet red by now.

Grayson slowly turned around to make eye contact with me again, the same amusement on his face but now joined by a hint of something else. Something that made my heart flutter.

Attraction? Was it reciprocal? I mean, it sure seemed that way. But I could talk or think myself out of any good conclusion if I let my mind dwell on the subject. I tried to remind myself that it didn't matter what this gorgeous hunk of muscle thought about me. He wasn't one of my clients or photographers. He was just the big, buff, heroic pilot who emerged from out of nowhere to rescue us and salvage what we could of this photoshoot disaster. So yeah, it was a little hard not to feel indebted to him, really. I owed him a lot already, and it didn't help that he was stunningly easy on the eyes.

And that take-charge attitude he displayed intrigued me. I was such a control freak that I had always steered clear of dating other assertive guys. I always ended up being the one with the upper hand. Never in a toxic or unequal way, just that the guys who were usually into me liked me for my type A demeanor. Therefore, they were looking for someone to motivate them and give them advice, nudge them along through life. Sometimes, my brief forays into dating had felt more like freelance life-coaching. The sort of men who gravitated to me were generally feeling unmoored in some part of their lives. They looked to me to stabilize them, to make their life feel organized amid the chaos of the modern world. And for the most part, I had leaned into that persona. I had allowed myself to "pick up strays", as my colleagues always said, taking in guys with rough pasts or aimless ambitions. I was good at helping people define their goals and follow through on them. It was a skill I had spent years and years honing in this go-go-go industry. Some of my friends thought I was being taken advantage of, that I was pouring too much of my already-spread-thin energy on people who were incapable of reciprocating in the same fashion. And they were right about that. It was a rut I fell into again and again. In fact, it was partly because of that rut that I decided to pursue a new, exciting life here in Alaska. I wanted to shake out all the skeletons in my closet, cut out the unnecessary distractions, and follow my heart for once. Since my company wanted to open a new branch in Anchorage and had its eyes on me as the man to run it, this was the perfect chance to test the waters.

Of course, I had never expected my heart to wander anywhere near a guy like Grayson, but here we were. No denying the butterflies in my stomach or the rapid gallop of my heart. As I watched Grayson peel off his shirt and put on a different one, better suited to the task of going to the gym, I found myself getting lost in the beauty of his shape. He had scars here and there, nothing too dramatic, just enough to interest me and show how much he had endured. I knew each and every one of those marks came with a story attached, and I found myself desperately wishing for some quiet, private, golden moments with Grayson's body just so I could learn every individual tale. I wanted to memorize every story in the whorl of my fingertips, imprint every inch of his glorious body to my recollection forever. He was one of a kind, and he was right in front of me. Seeing the aurora borealis in the sky could not have been a more mesmerizing sight to behold than Grayson simply changing clothes.

He came and sat next to me on the edge of the bed while he pulled on socks and some athletic sneakers, lacing them up tightly. I felt all tingly and warm inside just from sitting so close to him, feeling the heat coming off his perfect body in waves, the faint scent of his masculinity, the soft, rhythmic sounds of his breath. I almost felt giddy, like a kid in a candy shop or a drunk in a bar. Like I was so close to the sweetness, the satisfaction I craved. Grayson was just so much man. I only hoped I could be good enough to deserve all of what he had to offer. I was sure as hell willing to try my best. Grayson stood up and stretched, showing off every perfectly-toned muscle of his arms. I let out a low whistle, totally impressed.

"Careful, you might make my models look bad by comparison," I remarked.

He chuckled. "I don't think there's any risk of that," he replied humbly.

"Let's just hope they don't all lose their minds when you walk in," I said, getting up to follow him. He looked over at me with one brow arched. He looked so damn cute that way.

"Got some sensitive souls in there?" he joked.

"Oh yeah. Well, you know how it is. Everybody in the industry's just a little bit neurotic," I said. "But don't worry, some of them are actually a *lot* neurotic."

"But not you," he pointed out.

I could have melted through the floor. "Well, if you think I'm not neurotic, then I must be better at hiding my true feelings than I thought I was," I laughed.

"Ah, come on. You're put-together. I bet you were one of those kids who always colored within the lines in kindergarten, huh?" he teased.

I couldn't stop grinning like a fool. "Okay, you got me there. But who the hell colors outside the lines intentionally like some kind of madman?" I retorted.

"Life is about taking measured risks, Connor," Grayson answered with a surprising level of clarity and wisdom.

"Ooh, you're way better than a fortune cookie," I joked.

He nudged my arm with his bicep and I nearly went weak in the knees.

"Damn. That's harsh," he laughed. "I'm speaking the truth."

"Oh, I know. You're totally right," I assured him. "I just hope I measured out this risk properly. You know, coming all the way out to Alaska. Leaving everything behind. If things work out and I can move up to Anchorage after it's over, I don't want my first memory of this place to be... sour."

"You'll find your footing. I know you will," he said firmly.

And somehow, hearing those words in his authoritative, deep voice made it feel just a little closer to reality. A little truer. I smiled to myself as we walked into the gym, feeling a good bit lighter than I had all day.

The gym was absolutely mind-boggling. Every possible kind of equipment or tool was present. All items and designs were of the highest quality and the most durable, luxury materials. The mirrors were shiny and glossy, completely free of prints or streaks. Even the floor looked clean enough to eat from. I had been to a lot of gyms in my life, and I knew to expect some level of… well, not-great smells. Any location for which the sole purpose of its existence is to wring blood, sweat, and tears out of a human body would naturally pick up some unpleasant odors after some time. It was just the way of things.

But this place seemed brand new, like all this equipment had never before been touched by human hands. The only smell currently was the soft fragrance of a citrusy disinfectant product and the mingled faint scents of the models gathered in the room. Many of them wore cologne, even to a shoot in a fitness setting, probably as a way of inducing calmness or confidence. I didn't blame them. It took a lot of guts to get in front of a camera for any reason, much more to do so when your image was going to be plastered all over billboards, magazines, and of course the ubiquitous internet. Each model had his own ritual or pre-shoot routine to get them feeling pumped up and ready to pose and look perfect on demand for hours on end.

As expected, the models gathered in the gym all gave Grayson an impressed double take, as they clearly hadn't expected to see so much of his perfect body walk into the room. He was wearing exercise joggers and an athletic-wear t-shirt, nothing too revealing or special. But there was just something about Grayson that drew the eye. He was striking to look at, and the calm, powerful aura he emitted certainly added to the overall mystique and intrigue of his persona. People paid attention to him. They couldn't help it. Whenever he was in the room, he was the brightest shining light. Then again, perhaps I was just a little bit biased.

To my relief, though, the models quickly moved on from their momentary crises of jealousy or confusion at Grayson's appearance. They assembled themselves with the appropriate gear and equipment befitting their respective levels of strength, endurance, flexibility—all that jazz. The bulky bodybuilder types gathered in the weightlifting area. The tall, lean models took to the treadmills and workout machines. Niko and Erik got comfortable in the little yoga studio section of the gym. As I looked around, I couldn't help but feel a little thrill of relief and even excitement. There seemed to be something for everyone. Including Grayson. I was amused and impressed to find him slip into place alongside the other weightlifters. He encouraged the models, helping spot them and teaching them better techniques while I stood nearby, totally in awe.

"Wow, were you a personal trainer in a past life or something?" I joked.

He glanced over at me with glittering eyes and ruddy cheeks from exertion. He looked so delicious my brain actually stopped manufacturing thoughts for a full second or so. Then he laughed and gave me a shrug.

"I'm a pilot. It's important for me to stay in good shape, especially out here in the bush. So the guys and I tend to spend a lot of hours putting in work at the gym," he said. "I've picked up a lot of helpful information that way."

"I'll say. I had no idea my form was off all this time," said Tomas. "I've been in and out of the ring for years and never had a coach fix my posture to be just right."

"Don't mention it. I just wish you'd found out about it sooner. Probably would have saved you some pain," Grayson replied, sounding for all the world like someone's clever older brother or maybe a hot, wise father…

Here I was, letting my lust get the best of me again. As I watched Grayson coach the models and help them maximize productivity in their workouts, my heart swelled with affection and warmth for him. It was a truly lovely sight to behold. The models, who could admittedly be a little uptight at times, were starting to relax. Grayson just had that kind of a presence: calming, reassuring. You could trust his words and his intentions. His goodness glowed from within.

"Hey Connor!" he said suddenly, bringing me back to reality. "Spot me, will you?"

"Oh! Sure, of course," I said, rushing over to help him as he impressively lifted an absolutely monstrous barbell.

The models all whistled and clapped with amazement, but Grayson's demeanor remained humble. He thanked everyone and then moved on to the next little group of models in their zones. I followed after him like a lovesick puppy, just watching him lean into the role of gym liaison. He instructed the models on how to properly use the equipment and get the most out of their exercise while I watched with hearts in my eyes. He had warmed to the leadership role and the models had warmed to him, but there was still something nagging at the back of my mind.

I tried to whisper to Grayson aside, "What do I tell the photographers?"

He shrugged and dismissed the issue, replying softly, "Don't worry about the photographers just yet. That outdoor shoot is not going to happen anytime soon, judging by the weather. But these models came for a workout, so we're going to give them one."

"But what about afterward? The photographers are just standing around," I said.

"I know. But you have to be patient. Things will fall into place," he assured me.

He continued to do much of the same, going from group to group and distributing tips and advice to help them maximize their workouts most effectively. I was starting to wonder if there was anything in this world Grayson *didn't* know how to do.

"You're a true Renaissance man," I commented, watching him pull off some seriously dodgy yoga poses alongside Niko and Erik.

"I get around," he joked back.

I laughed, even as my face burned pink. I watched with amusement as Grayson's big, bulky body pretzeled itself into the same shapes that the much slimmer Niko and Erik were attempting. They were mismatched, and it was easy to pick out which one didn't quite belong there. But Grayson did more than just hold his own—he excelled. Physically, he seemed to know how to make his body do whatever he wanted it to. That was pretty mind blowing to me, considering how much coercion and psyching myself up I had to do in order to just get a good solid jog around the neighborhood out of my body.

Once the workout was winding down to the end, Grayson surprised me again by pulling the photographers aside with me. They looked eager to hear what he had to say.

"Okay. So, you guys understand that the outdoor shoot you had in mind is off the table, correct?" he began.

"Unfortunately, yeah," said Chuck.

"Well, I have another idea for you," he said. "The gym. You saw the way all these guys looked at home doing their usual workouts. This gym has every piece of equipment you could possibly need. There's a boxing ring down the hall. There's an indoor pool. Anything you need, we've got it. So here's my idea: you hold the photoshoot here in the gym."

"Hmm. It's interesting," said the other photographer, stroking his chin.

"Obviously, these guys all need to get cleaned up first, but what do you think?" Grayson asked, looking back and forth between them.

The photographers seemed to silently confer for a moment, then Chuck grinned.

"Yeah. You know what? Yeah. Let's do it. Worth a try, plus the lighting in here is surprisingly good for a gymnasium," he laughed.

The models were informed and headed off to shower and preen for the cameras. They came back, and each took turns using different areas of the gym while the photographers snapped photo after photo. All the while, Grayson did a great job of nudging the models and photographers alike into better positioning, better lighting, unconventional poses. It was exciting to watch. He was totally confident in everything he said and did, which I greatly admired.

However, I did have one problem: it was very, very hard not to just focus completely on Grayson. I knew I was supposed to be paying attention to the shoot, to the models themselves, to accommodating their needs. But Grayson was so damn hot, he might as well have been on fire. I couldn't take my eyes off him. I kept getting distracted and forgetting to do my job, as it was much more tantalizing to look at Grayson from across the room. All those hard muscles glistening and glowing with a faint sheen of sweat, the bright lights reflecting off his sculpted frame, almost putting the real models to shame. And after a while, it dawned on me that some of Grayson's actions were intentional. He was trying to get my attention. He was enjoying the privilege of being able to distract me and render me tongue-tied so effortlessly, and I had to admit that it kind of turned me on.

Okay, no. It super turned me on. To the point that, when the shoot was over, and Grayson came and told me we ought to hit the shower together, I thought my heart might burst out of my chest. I followed him, wide-eyed and slack-jawed down the hall, up the stairs, and off to the bathroom. I watched him strip out of his gym clothes and step into the steamy water, my mouth watering all the while. I could see his perfect body silhouetted through the curtain, my cock twitching with need.

"You coming?" he asked, poking his head out from behind the shower curtain.

"Oh. Yes!" I blurted out.

I hastily whipped off my clothes and climbed into the shower with Grayson, unable to hide the erection growing between my legs. He glanced down at my cock, then smirked.

"So, how was it?" he asked.

"How was what?" I replied, confused.

"Giving up the reins to someone else for a change," he elaborated.

"Oh, that. Well, I'll tell you the truth… it felt pretty good. Nerve wracking at first, but then good. You know what you're doing," I said. "It was kind of a relief, getting to stand by without shouldering the responsibility by myself. My job is hectic. I work hard and long hours. And dealing with the talent can be frustrating at times. Getting to see you take charge almost made this feel more like a vacation. A release."

Grayson stepped closer, his enormous, muscular frame towering over me. In a low, gravelly voice he growled, “How would you like to experience a *true* release?”

I looked up at him with a little tinge of defiance, egging him on. I wanted him to take charge. I wanted him to control me.

I smiled mischievously and said, “Show me what you’ve got.”

6

GRAYSON

THAT WAS ALL THE INVITATION I NEEDED.

I leaned—no, lunged forward and hugged him tight to me as I pressed a kiss not to his mouth, but to the soft, vulnerable neck he had exposed to me. Immediately, my shaft ground against the groove of the vee pointing from his abs to his crotch, and his slid against my slick, wet thigh. I leaned into him and pinned him against the cool tile walls and felt the hot water hitting my back and pouring down the ridges and valleys of my muscles in thin streams.

My hands went to his biceps, and I slowly ran them down the length of his arms. My fingers felt every detail, and I thought about every moment he had spent chiseling his body into shape. For a city boy, he knew how to keep his body toned. Maybe it was a perk of working alongside fitness models, or maybe Connor was just that kind of man.

I wanted to know every little detail about him. The craving for him had been eating me up all day, growing hotter and hotter every moment we spent together. I didn't know how much longer I could have lasted without dragging him off somewhere private to work out the tension that had been getting pulled tighter every passing hour.

"I want to be *crystal* clear about what I mean," I growled in the steam that clouded the shower stall.

When my hands reached his wrists, I pushed them back against the wall and held them there, exposing him completely to me. I looked down at him, watching those glistening eyes shine up at me in the misty air with rapt attention. He was exquisite.

"You've been pretty clear so far," he said with that petulant, challenging smirk that made me want to kiss it off of him.

"You like giving up control because you take on so much," I told him, squeezing his wrists and letting him feel that he was being held down. "You're good, but you need release. You need to give it up. I want to take that from you. But if you want to go there, I need you to surrender it to me."

The way I was speaking to Connor was pure bedroom talk, there was no question about my tone, and the fact that he could not only pick up on that immediately but also be so wholly, readily into it was more than I could have expected. Connor was lightning in a bottle, and I was going to hold the lid shut tight.

"What else could you possibly need to take from me?" he said, knowing full well how dangerous those words were. "You've got me up here, trapped, on the brink of a breakdown, and more exposed than I've been with anyone in… a very long time," he finished, biting his lip.

"That's just it," I said in an almost amused tone, running a hand through his short, wet hair and slowly curling it into a fist that I could use to tug his head back with. "There's only one thing left to surrender: you."

Connor licked his lips, and I felt his cock pulse against me.

"If you weren't here, I don't know what I'd be doing," he confessed. "I need you. You're right. I need *this*," he said, and he pushed his hips forward to let my cock grind harder against him.

It sent a ripple of sweet warmth up my body, and I closed my eyes for a moment to savor it. When I opened them again, I pushed back, pinning his entire body to the wall, overwhelming him with my size and making him feel smaller and more helpless than ever. I shifted our bodies and pushed a leg up just enough to push our two cocks together, and I started grinding them. The thick shafts of our manhood slid up and down, each pulsing with desire and flushed a dark tone that made them look that much more desperate for release.

"When we're together like this, your body is mine," I told him in that same tone I used to boss him around the lodge. "You follow my orders. You do as I say. If I want you to come when we're together, I might be generous and let you. If I don't, then you won't."

He swallowed and nodded his head. "Yes, sir."

"You're not used to men like me," I growled. "I'm going to show you how to please me. Are you ready to listen?"

"I am," he said, panting as I tormented his crotch with slow, steady grinding.

"Then we need a safe word," I said.

"Frigid," he said after half a moment's thought.

"That was quick," I remarked, chuckling.

"Ever since you shut that front door behind you yesterday," he said, averting his eyes, "things have been heating up in here. To tell you the truth, the cold's the furthest thing from my mind… thanks to you."

My cock ached as my balls felt so swollen with need that I could have unleashed myself right then and there. I reached down, finally releasing his wrists to take both of our cocks in one hand while sliding the other around to his ass and looking down at him ravenously.

"Frigid, then," I repeated, nodding in acknowledgment.

I started to slide my hand across the length of our shafts, and my rough knuckles pushed against his abs as I started working us together. I took my time at first, getting to know the shape of his cock and admiring the view from above. But before long, I grew more possessive.

"I want to feel you," I growled before I spun him around so that his front faced the wall. "And I want to know exactly what kind of body I have on my hands."

"I can't hide anything from you," he confessed. "I'm yours. Every inch. Don't hold back."

"If I didn't have perfect discipline over my body," I growled, "I couldn't even if I wanted to. Your lucky day."

He shivered, and I slid my finger between the firm cheeks of his ass until I found his hole. My pointer finger brushed against it, and I felt just how tight he was going to feel. My cock grew even harder, and Connor could tell. He arched his back to offer up more of himself to my relentless hands. As I felt the warmth roll up the trunk of my shaft and through my body, I imagined how much more intense it was for Connor.

When a man handled himself, there were ways he unconsciously betrayed himself—you know your own natural rhythm, so you can only feel so good touching yourself. But with another man's hand working you, knowing every intimate detail of male sexuality from firsthand experience but having none of the experience to dull the thrill? That was a sweet thought indeed and thinking about what kind of bliss Connor was feeling made it all the better.

I liked a willing submissive. I wanted to bend him to my will in every way, but having it offered up was even sweeter. *Connor* made it sweeter.

His face was pressed against the spotless, smooth wall as I dragged my teeth across his neck. One hand teased the outside of his hole while the other stroked his shaft vigorously, picking up speed. But every time I sensed him getting too wound up down there, I took a well-timed detour to his balls to feel how heavy and needy they were. When I came, I sometimes felt like all the stress and tension of life was getting washed out of me, literally. I wanted that for Connor. I wanted to connect with him in the way our bodies felt, to resonate with this near-captive man on one more level.

Sex didn't get me thinking so deeply that often, but something about Connor drew it out.

My finger had been making a slow, steady trek around the edge of Connor's tightness, teasing him so deliciously it was almost too good to move on from. But my patience wore out, and at last, I slipped that finger into him. Connor drew in a hissing breath as I teased the skin of his neck between my teeth, then moved my mouth up to nip the bud of his ear. Every shiver and twitch I felt from him was ecstatic to me.

The bold finger worked its way in and swirled around the rim, getting it ready for the second thick finger that joined it. Connor's mouth fell open, and I turned his body around, fingers still in his ass like a hook. I covered his mouth with a kiss as my fingers started massaging him from within. He moaned, and I pushed my tongue against his. My hand picked back up a steady pace on his cock. I was in two of his holes, and I had his manhood in my grasp—to say Connor had given himself up to me would be an understatement.

But there was one more way he could do that.

I felt him grow tighter between his legs until I knew that any more pushing would spill him.

"You feel that?" I growled, brushing my thumb over the tip of his cock and smiling ruthlessly. "That fire inside your shaft, burning to get out? You want me to free that for you?"

"Yes, sir," he begged me. "Please, I can't do it without you. I can't do anything without you right now. You're the only one who can pour me out."

"Damn right," I growled, and my hand froze on his cock.

Connor gasped, and a spurt of precome escaped him. If my thumb hadn't been up against his very tip, I wouldn't have even noticed in the hot shower.

"Shit," he gasped, smiling and blushing. "Maybe closer than I thought."

I slid my fingers out of him and picked him up abruptly, making him yelp. There was something empowering about easily handling a man who was already fit and sturdy in his own right. I carried him out of the shower, and I set him down to let him towel me off. I spread my arms like a statue, watching him almost reverently dry my warm skin. When he was finished, I grabbed him and gruffly scrubbed him dry as well before hauling him into the bedroom, nostrils flaring like a bull's.

He rolled on the bed when I thrust him down on it and licked my lips, flexing my hands. I strode to the nightstand, took out a condom, slipped one on, and used the lube Connor packed to prepare myself as he got on his knees for me.

I approached him and grabbed his ass, glaring at its tempting, firm, round shape and feeling how smooth his skin was. I'd never wanted to claim something so badly. But out of the corner of my eye, I spotted something else in Connor's suite that had piqued my curiosity.

It was a large, luxurious armchair, the kind you'd expect to see in some fancy British drawing room. It faced the window, and at that moment, I knew what I wanted. Smirking down at Connor, I shook my head.

"Not here," I rumbled.

Before he could answer, I scooped him up once again. It was aggressive, but Connor had to fight not to laugh, the chemistry between us had grown so fluid and natural. I felt like I was acting out fantasies I'd only imagined, and Connor had been tailor-made for me.

I sat down on the armchair and felt my massive frame sink perfectly into it. It suited me, and the smell of rich leather filled my nostrils as I perched Connor on top of my cock.

"Oh, fuck," Connor groaned as he felt my cock push at his entrance.

"Let me in, Connor," I growled. "Now."

I lowered him ever so slightly, and my cock entered him. The heat that ran up my body was almost scalding. The hole I'd felt with my fingers so thoroughly was even tighter around my crown, but with a little persistence, I started working him over me like a sleeve. I groaned as my powerful arms held his body in my complete power. He couldn't so much as squirm without my permission.

"Realized you're in over your head yet?" I asked.

"I just… I just slipped past your head," he panted with a mischievous smile on his face.

I snorted.

"You'll pay for that one, smartass," I growled, and I slid him so far down on my cock that we both let out tense, desperate moans while I felt my vein-ribbed cock growing more swollen and ready.

My cock glided back and forth, pounding his inner depths with the sturdy grip of my own two hands holding him up. Connor's hands were on the arms of the chair, but he barely needed to touch it. Any burn I felt in my arms was too delicious to give up, all because of what I was working toward.

I didn't want to wait much longer. My body demanded release, and it had earned its reward. I let Connor support himself just enough for me to sacrifice a hand… bringing it to his cock and leaning him against a thigh as I thrust up into him.

"You will come with me," I growled as a clear, explicit order. "And you'll call my name."

"Yes, sir," he groaned.

I started pumping into him relentlessly. My shaft was a force of nature, pistoning into him with more precision than I'd ever used for anyone. I couldn't explain what it was about this man that drove me to push myself like that, but I leaned into it. I followed my instincts. And my instincts honed in on Connor.

The masculine scent in the air drove me harder and harder onward while my hand groped and massaged Connor's shaft. He was trying to keep up with my orders, but I was making it hard on him as well as in him. My bulging crown massaged his innermost sanctuary, and finally, the searing fire couldn't stay back any longer.

I let out a hoarse groan as I came, and at the same time, Connor let out a burst of come that hit his chest. We pulsed and emptied ourselves together, staring out the foggy window to the inky blackness beyond. I felt pure, blissful ecstasy surging through my body as my release washed over me. It dazed me. I'd never felt anything like it, and my body felt as though it had awoken something new and beautifully dangerous.

And then, the pulsing slowed, and the fierce, masculine rutting melted into gentler cuddling. I hugged him to me while I was still lodged inside him, and I felt his come running over my fingers as I juiced the last of him. He let out a murmuring sigh with one last shiver and spurt, and we were spent.

"That," I said in a husky tone, "is what you're getting this week, if you obey me," I demanded of him.

"I will," he breathed, panting. "I… I'm yours, Grayson."

A hungry smile crossed my lips.

This week was going to suit me just fine.

7

CONNOR

It was a gorgeous day here in rural Alaska, and the heavy, punishing snowfall of the past couple days had wound down to a much softer, more whimsical flurry. It was still keeping us snowed in, but the world outside looked more like a wonderland than a wasteland now. And it was especially beautiful to behold from my current vantage point, sitting in the bleachers of the indoor pool at our private luxury lodge. The pool was well-heated, the whole place environmentally sealed and regulated for temperature and humidity. The ladder rose high up, high enough for a diving board to cast its long, narrow shadow across the pool. The walls had massive, glossy windows through which one could see a veritable landscape of flora and fauna.

Even though it was still frigidly cold outside, the world was blanketed in fluffy white snow that gave it all an unearthly glow. The evergreens stretched high up toward the sky, unfazed by the harsh winter, whereas many other deciduous trees fell bare and barren. They looked a bit like scrawny bodies standing outside and stretching their knobby limbs out. The sky was still that sort of grayish color I assumed did not go away until the summer finally arrived, but there was a hint of blue underneath that. I could tell that if not for the cold and the heavy accumulation of snowfall, it would have been a lovely day to go out for a nice hike.

But it was nice in here, too. I was having a surprisingly relaxing time watching my model clients swimming and diving in the pool, enjoying themselves and working out their stiff limbs after a hard sleep last night. The photoshoot in the gym had tired everybody out, so this morning had been a little slow-moving. But by now, mid-morning, everyone seemed to be in a light, cheery mood. The weather had let up a little, and the heated pool was undoubtedly working wonders for their sore muscles.

I loved to swim, but I didn't feel as safe swimming around in there with them. I knew it was just a side effect of being a control freak, but I tended to worry about my models' safety a lot. Not because any of them were especially high-risk or reckless; in fact, they all took damn good care of themselves and had their heads on straight. But I preferred to perch up here at the top of the bleachers, with a near bird's eye view of the activities happening below. I could watch all my little chickadees in a row, keeping an eye on them. Sometimes I wondered if there was some kind of gentle parental energy I was trying to work out on them, but oh well. I chalked it up to professional courtesy. They counted on me to look out for them in professional situations, but I couldn't just do that. I took everything personally. I poured my whole self into my line of work, and if that meant watching them all swim in the heated luxury pool like I was a lifeguard at a summer camp for exceptionally cute kids, then so be it.

In fact, I was feeling pretty good. On top of my game, actually. My two photographers were pleased with how the gymnasium shoot had gone yesterday, and they were now scheming a few rows down from me about turning the pool area into a shoot, as well. The creative juices were definitely flowing, and I had Grayson to thank for that.

"Ooh, and the bluish tones of the water would contrast so beautifully with the greenery outside," Chuck was saying.

"And the snow," David added, nodding. "It's weird, isn't it? The lighting here?"

"I know. It's better than I expected, especially with the snow,"

Chuck replied. He glanced over at me with a wry smile. "You did good, Connor. This place is fantastic."

"Thanks, man," I replied. "I'm just relieved to see it all coming together. I know this wasn't the ideal situation, but I feel like we're really making the best of it."

"Yeah, and that hot pilot certainly makes it easier, eh?" he teased, giving me a wink.

I rolled my eyes, hoping they couldn't hear the way my heart started racing. All it took was just the mention of Grayson's name, and my mind would drift away. I was daydreaming about him while the photographers started discussing techniques and which lenses to employ for the shoot. They prepared themselves and headed down the bleachers to start setting up cameras. I rested my chin on my hand, smiling contentedly as I watched the scene unfolding.

Chuck and David set up the lighting, the focus, the angles—they bounced ideas off of one another and egged each other on. I loved watching them work—it was another symbiotic relationship playing out, both of them very different artists with different perspectives, and yet they seamlessly wove in and out of the scene together. They had different styles, David giving precise instructions on pose, expression, mood—and Chuck preferring to take a more laissez-faire approach. David was hyper-critical of his work even during the scene, though he was luckily quick to reassure the model he was doing great. Chuck shouted out compliments and expressions of excitement throughout the shoot.

Models responded in a variety of ways, some preferring David's tendency to instruct and guide, while others liked how positive and vocal Chuck was. David was photographing the guys gathered in the shallow end where they could all gaze moodily into the camera lens, their cut upper bodies on display. Chuck had a flair for the dynamic, so he took lots of action shots. The bravest and most water-savvy of the models posed on the diving board and performed dives for him. Both photographers took some seriously beautiful shots of water droplets and sweat mingling on Diego's forehead as he backstroked across the pool. There were shots of Erik, champion swimmer, shooting through the water so quickly that his body was basically a hydrodynamic blur, and Niko's glorious, shaggy blond hair snapping up in a crest of golden light and spray as he emerged from underwater, his lips slightly parted in a soft gasp.

Everyone on both sides of the camera lens was killing it. The models were so comfortable and at home in the heated water, able to swim and be playful, working out their pent-up energy and showing more authentic smiles. They loosened up and tried more daring poses and expressions, lending the shoot an abundance of variety. The photographers picked up on the cheerful mood of the models, letting it feed their creativity as they worked. And I, of course, stood back and enjoyed the show, content in the fact that there was nothing anybody really needed from me.

For once, I was kind of okay with that. Most of the time, with my personality, I was dying for someone to need me, to ask me for advice. I genuinely loved coaching people, helping them reach their goals. I was good at disentangling hectic schedules and restoring order to chaos. Being needed made me feel more confident in my skills. But today, I felt just fine. The view from the bleachers was breathtaking, and the vibe in the gigantic indoor pool facility was light and bouncy. All was well, for the moment, at least.

Satisfied that everyone was doing well down there without my assistance, I began to relax and start looking around. The facilities here really were spectacular. I couldn't imagine that this place ever got busy enough to fill up the indoor pool, but I was grateful for having it. A heated pool was a perfect respite from the cold, and a departure from the norm as far as photoshoots went. Apart from the models who were known best as swimmers, like Erik, they were used to posing in much drier locations. But this snow-in had definitely pushed us all in creativity. As it turned out, you could make just about anything work when it came right down to it. I was learning to let go of my biases, slowly but surely, and just go with the flow. Sometimes. Not always, but sometimes.

My eyes continued looking around the room, following the neat parallel lines of the wooden beams across the ceiling, until I caught sight of something that made me do a double take. Up on the second floor, there was a big, wide-pane window showing the comfy, cozy luxury coffeehouse there, and sitting at a table right in the center of the window was Grayson. He looked almost comically out of place, his gruff appearance contrasting sharply with the soft and cushy atmosphere of the cafe. I had to put a hand over my mouth to stifle a laugh. He wasn't looking my way, and I squinted to see that he seemed to be talking to someone across the table from him, but the angle kept me from seeing the other guy. I needed to be up there. Besides, I hadn't had my coffee yet.

I looked back at the shoot unfolding in front of me, making sure things were still going well. They were. Definitely. Everyone was smiling, splashing each other, having a good time. And at the moment, they didn't exactly need me to be there, so...

I got up, gave a nod to Chuck and David, and headed for the stairs. I felt almost as though an unseen force was picking me up and carrying me in this direction, like the hand of fate itself was in control. I had no idea what I was going to do or say once I got up to the cafe, but I knew with every thread of my being that I needed to go to wherever Grayson was. If he was there, it was the place to be. Simple as that. It didn't make any sense, but with every step I took, my heart pounded harder, the butterflies having some kind of obscene rave in my stomach. I stepped up onto the second floor and looked over, realizing with some concern that Grayson's cafe companion was Landon, the other pilot. Therefore, they had more in common than I had with Grayson. They were probably discussing something important, something professional, and here I was about to strut up to them and ruin it. My hands felt clammy as I walked up to the table, my throat going dry. I felt like I was back in high school, just an awkward teen approaching the lunch table of the gorgeous jock a million light years out of my league. And yet, I could not stay away. Not even if I'd wanted to. But as I walked up to him, I was relieved to see the way Grayson's eyes lit up instantly. The weight shifted off my shoulders and I felt light as air.

"Connor," Grayson greeted me with a nod.

Landon turned to look at me, grinning broadly. "Oh, hey man! How's it going down there?"

"Surprisingly great. I think everyone needed a bit of a break, so it's like a vacation and a photoshoot at the same time," I explained. "Should get some great shots out of it. I just hope none of the equipment falls into the pool or anything."

"Nah, those guys have it under control," Landon assured me. He looked back to Grayson and said brightly, "Well, I'd better get going. You two have at it."

"Oh, you don't have to go," I said, hoping I sounded more sincere than I felt. I really liked Landon, but the idea of getting another moment alone with Grayson was so delicious.

"No worries! I'll catch up with you guys later. I'm off to watch the shoot," Landon said.

He hopped up and walked off, leaving it free for me to slide into the seat across from Grayson. He was looking at me with those gorgeous eyes gently blazing. I could almost smell the desire on him, and it was intoxicating. He wanted me? He wanted to be alone with me? I could sense, despite my self-deprecation and disbelief, that it was true. I rushed to find something to say.

"So, I wanted to thank you," I said, smiling.

He tilted his head. "Thank me for what?"

"For the idea of doing that gym shoot yesterday. Not only did that one go off without a hitch, it helped inspire today's pool shoot. We're getting a great variety of shots, thanks to you," I told him.

"Well, you're welcome," he replied gruffly. "Not too often I get to think artistically with my job, but it's been an interesting experience working with you all."

"Yeah, I bet your job is a lot more... serious," I said.

He snorted. "Sometimes, yes. But your job is worthwhile, too, Connor. You make art. Art makes life good. Right?" he pointed out.

I blushed. "I guess you're right. Yeah."

"Besides, it's a nice break from the usual grind. You know, I've been doing this pilot thing for a while now. It never gets old, though," he mused. "Started this company up with my buddies Daniel and Caleb as soon as we got our pilot licenses. Picked out the land we wanted and built from the ground up. In Anchorage, because we needed to be centrally located, but still on the outskirts of town to maintain that peace and quiet we liked. We would be our own bosses. We would take on a lot of responsibility. It was a tall order. We were just kids then, chasing this big dream. Still can't believe it sometimes, that we managed to catch it."

"This whole place is like a dream to me," I admitted. "I mean, everywhere you look is more beauty. It's all so wild. It feels... somehow both impossible and more real than anything I've ever experienced. I'm glad I'm here."

"I'm glad you're here, too," Grayson said.

"The feeling is mutual," I said softly. Worried that I'd pushed too far, I backpedaled to our more professional topic. "You know, I'm actually moving to Anchorage after this excursion is over."

He looked genuinely surprised—in a good way. That warmed my heart. He smirked.

"You're coming to my turf, huh?" he teased.

"You got it," I laughed. "That's why I was selected for this week-long shoot: my company is promoting me to a higher paid position in the agency's new Anchorage branch."

Grayson's eyes were shining. The bright light spilling in through the windows cast him in a heavenly glow. I felt almost star-struck.

"You'll be so happy in Anchorage," he said. "I just know it. The city's great. Don't get me wrong, I love the rural parts of my home state so much, but if you have to live in a city, it may as well be Anchorage. Great food, fantastic art and culture, beautiful sights—there's always something fun going on. You'll fit in there great."

"Maybe you can show me around sometime," I suggested bravely.

He looked at me hard, and for a moment I thought he was offended by my forwardness. But just as the panic was starting to pick up, he reached his foot over to mine underneath the table. I froze up, watching the light flicker in his eyes as his lips curled into a devilish, almost predatory smile. He leaned in slowly and I did the same, hardly daring to breathe. I watched his mouth open, and the hottest words I had ever heard came spilling out in a breathy growl.

"I have something to show you right now, if you're eager to learn."

The hairs on the back of my neck stood up and goosebumps prickled up along my skin. I was so flooded with arousal and surprise that I could hardly choke out an "uh-huh" before Grayson nodded for me to get up and follow him. Almost as though in a trance, I rose and trailed after him, my eyes locked onto him like he might disappear into a dream world at any moment. To my confusion, he led me behind the bar counter of the utterly empty cafe.

"The guys have taken a liking to the cafe, but we might have a few minutes of privacy, Grayson whispered, starting to unzip his jeans.

I dropped to my knees, my heart racing like crazy.

"Think we have time?" I murmured, looking up at him.

He nodded and smirked. "You up for the challenge?"

I wrapped a hand around his thick, hard cock and nodded, grinning with anticipation. I decided the best answer was to just get started. I spread my mouth open and pulled his hard shaft between my lips, flicking my tongue around the engorged head while my hand worked his length. Immediately, Grayson began entangling his fingers in my hair, holding my head in place. His hips reared back and pistoned forward, his cock shoving to the back of my throat. I started to gag but managed to stop myself, my eyes burning as Grayson groaned appreciatively.

"Fuck, that's hot," he growled.

Encouraged and turned on by the force with which he needed me, I began to suck his cock harder, barely letting myself have room to breathe as he fucked my mouth. I groaned, my own cock twitching between my legs.

"Don't touch yourself. There's no time now," he ordered between clenched teeth. "Later."

I moaned in agreement, sending vibrations through his core. Grayson tilted his head back and thrust his hips forward, in and out, fucking my throat. Our time was ticking by quickly, and I knew if we didn't finish soon, we would undoubtedly get caught. But knowing that didn't scare me. It just made me more determined. I had a goal—to get him off as fast as possible. So I gave it my all, pumping his cock in and out of my mouth, flicking my tongue, moaning and twisting to give him every angle of pleasure. He gripped the back of my head, grunting as his body stiffened. His thrusts became more and more erratic until finally he seized up and held me in place while his hard cock twitched in my mouth. His hot, salty seed slid down my throat and I gulped it down eagerly, cleaning up every last drop. By the time I opened my eyes to see that our time was up, it was over. Grayson stepped back, zipped his jeans, and pretended to be grabbing a cup of water. At the exact same time, I stood up and stepped out from behind the bar counter, facing away as though I wasn't even paying attention.

Moments later, one of the models came into the cafe with an innocent look on his face as he nodded to us, and I couldn't help but think how lucky we were. We'd cut it so close, but now Grayson was smirking at me as though I had just won a marathon. I could still taste him on my tongue when he walked by me to leave. As he passed, he whispered to me.

"Go back downstairs to the shoot," he commanded. "We'll pick up later."

I watched him disappear, totally awed. Then, I did exactly as I was told.

8

GRAYSON

THAT NIGHT, I SWUNG OPEN THE HATCH DOOR TO ONE OF THE LODGE'S turrets, which led to the exposed stone gazebo that topped the little tower. Landon and I had already cleared the snow off the turrets, because about an hour ago the snowfall had finally stopped. And that had given Connor and me an idea.

I stepped up into the chilly night's air, a heavy jacket over my shoulders, and I got to work starting the fire while the others spilled out behind me, most of them talking and laughing with each other, but that changed as soon as the air hit them. One by one, the models gave an almost uniform shiver as they piled out onto the relatively small space. They crowded the benches immediately, which some of them regretted when they felt how cold they were, but that changed in a matter of minutes.

I got the fire going, and I was pleased to see this lodge had planned for its cozy turret fires to spoil its guests. The fire pit was large, and the heat that traveled up got trapped in the gazebo just enough to slowly fill the space with an orb of warmth. Even the winds were being gracious to us tonight.

"Wow," Connor breathed as he stepped out last, after the cameramen. "Maybe I shouldn't have been so quick to curse our luck."

I'd been all over the state, but the view really was something. It was endless, untouched snowy mountains and inky black night skies lit up by a shining moon that made it look downright ethereal. The models were doing their best to appreciate it, too, but they were a little distracted by each other.

Once everyone was up on the patio, we were crowded in like sardines.

"So, I liked your idea about the gazebo shoot a lot, honestly," said David, one of the photographers. "But now that I'm actually standing here…"

"Crowded," said Niko plaintively.

"Si," Diego echoed.

"Normally that's not a problem, we can do some pretty surprising things with the right angles," David said, nodding, "but this is going to get a little awkward if we're shuffling this many people around all the time. Especially once we get the lighting equipment up here."

Connor frowned and tapped his chin, peering around at the group while I scratched my chin thoughtfully. They had a point, it would be hard and time-consuming to do one long shoot up here. The idea was to have the guys in kind of a relaxed situation, like telling stories around a fire like this, and when we saw that the snowfall was clearing up, we couldn't resist taking advantage of being outdoors.

A spark of light caught my attention, and I looked over the rooftop of the lodge to see Landon lighting up a second fire on the other turret, having just finished clearing it out. I smiled and looked at Connor, making eye contact and nodding toward the other tower. Connor followed my gaze, and his face brightened up.

"Okay," he said, turning to the photographers. "Do you have enough lighting equipment to do two shots at once?"

"Sure," David said, nodding to his colleague.

"Then I think Grayson and I just had an idea," he said, giving me a boyish grin.

Fifteen minutes later, half of the models were comfortably under one of the gazebos, with the other half at the second. A photographer had taken each group and gotten them outfitted in a few brands that they needed to advertise, and while all that took place, Connor and I made our way to a balcony where we could see both of the turrets—at least partly.

Connor was wearing a thick, cozy jacket and a sweater beneath it, and even so, I wanted to wrap my arms around him as he stepped to the railing and peered over to look at both of the photoshoots in progress. He laughed and waved to one of the models who acknowledged him, and when I got a look at the scene, I couldn't help but feel a smile tug at my lips too.

On one of the gazebos, two of the models were posing as if they were having a lively conversation with a couple of mugs of hot chocolate in hand. On the other scene, three of the models were leaning close to each other and looking very serious, as if they were having a sincere heart to heart. All around them, the photographers had set up some mess of lighting equipment I didn't want to even try to figure out, and the models who were "on deck" waiting were holding their own props. One had a book he was unknowingly holding upside-down, another had supplies for s'mores, and another had inexplicably brought a dumbbell.

As I watched everything unfolding and hugged Connor from behind, I felt a laugh building in my chest. Connor smiled and turned his head to look at me as I started chuckling, and the more I tried to stop, the louder it got. My voice was naturally deep, and I felt my chest reverberate against Connor as he turned his body the rest of the way around to face me.

"What's gotten into you?" he asked, grinning. "Excited as I am that this is working out? Because I'm pretty damn excited."

"No, it's just," I said, wiping an eye. "Something about the way they've got half a kitchen and a wardrobe up there like a movie set. And we just split them up and deployed them like they're some kind of... I dunno, private army of models," I said, letting out a final snicker.

"Oh, we could take over the town with this bunch, no doubt," Connor said, playing along with a grin. "New plan, instead of a photoshoot, we just squat the lodge. If they want to take it from us, they'll have to pry it from their beautiful, manicured hands!"

I pecked Connor on the cheek and chuckled as I turned him back around and hugged him against me, watching the photoshoot unfold.

"They're alright though when you get to know them," Connor said, leaning back into me. "I mean, I'm not exactly close friends with any of this group—no offense to them—they're professionals. They get the results we need, and that's all we need to worry about."

"You give them a lot of freedom, hm?" I asked, pushing my hips against his subtly. "I do things a little differently. I prefer a more hands-on approach. Keep my people on a short leash," I said, sliding my hands down to his crotch and warming it.

His shaft swelled and pulsed at my touch. He practically reacted on command. That was good. I would need him to be obedient for this.

"O-oh," he said, surprised but excited at the same time. "Okay. We... might be a little exposed here, don't you think?"

"What, are you shy?" I teased him, turning him around and taking him by the collar.

I pulled him close and smirked in his face, watching the reflection of the lights in his glimmering eyes. They looked full of wonder and fear, and even I had to admit that I was being more brash than usual. Any one of the crew up on the gazebos could have looked over and seen us but judging by the fact that I hadn't heard a shocked gasp yet, they either hadn't seen yet or didn't care. I couldn't lie—the risk that they might see us just added to the thrill.

"What if I want them to see?" I growled into his ear, sending goosebumps up the back of his neck. "I wouldn't mind showing you off to them. It would assure them you're in good hands," I said, and I spun Connor around to walk him back and pin him against the glass doors of the balcony.

They rattled, but almost everyone who was present at the lodge besides maybe an elusive employee was up and outside. Still, it felt so brazen to press a kiss to his lips and cup his face in my hands as I ground my hips against his. I drew the cold air into my lungs, and I let it out warm over Connor's face as our tongues danced. I chuckled through the kiss, feeling my shaft growing hard under my thick pants. Connor panted when the kiss broke, and he glanced anxiously over my shoulder to make sure nobody had seen.

"I was hoping to get you alone sometime tonight," I growled.

"You knew we had to do the shoot," Connor said with a teasing tone.

"Yeah," I grunted. "So I like distracting you. Big news. You owe me your attention when I demand it. You know that, don't you?"

The question in my tone was implied: if Connor wanted to play along, now was the time to let me know. But if he truly didn't want to risk getting caught, I could respect that. This shoot was important to him, and he knew his coworkers better than I did. I knew I was taking a risk when I dragged him across the balcony.

I'd never been afraid of risks. Taking risks was the only way to get a worthwhile reward.

But Connor never seemed to disappoint. That was intentional. He was the kind of man who never wanted to look bad, not because he was selfish, but because he wanted people to be able to rely on him when they needed to. It was a lot of pressure. I knew it all too well.

This was my way of relieving that pressure—for both of us.

"Yes, sir," he breathed.

"Good," I growled, and I looked to my left.

There was a small alcove where the wooden half-wall along the balcony became a full wall, probably a place to store the deck furniture when the winds were bad. For now, it would serve my purposes nicely.

I pushed his hands out of the way and slipped his jacket off his shoulders. He licked his lips as he watched me throw his jacket to the ground as padding for his knees, and I pointed to it with flared nostrils and a hard glare.

"On your knees," I commanded him, putting one trunk-like arm against the wall to his side. "Now."

Connor swallowed and nodded, slowly sinking to his knees on the gorgeous wooden balcony floor, eyes on the bulging outline of my manhood. He revered it like a prize, and his hands went to my thighs greedily. I caught his wrists and snorted, getting his attention.

"Belt," I grunted.

Connor nodded hastily, and I released his wrists to let him reach up and slide the strip of leather open and off of me before unbuttoning my pants. I reached down and took his hair in one of my hands, first running my fingers through it before taking a gentle but firm grip to let him know that I had control of the situation, no matter what.

"Take it in your hands," I rumbled. "Feel its weight."

Connor pulled my pants down just enough to let my thick trunk spring forth. It nearly smacked him in the face, and I couldn't help but chuckle as I pulled his mouth up against my crown. He groaned as his own shaft pushed against the inside of his pants. I pressed Connor to taste my cock, and he loved every moment of it. He slid his hands around to my ass and used it to hold on as he opened his mouth and took the crown in.

His tongue bathed the tip of my cock in warmth, a welcome change after the chilly air. Between our shared body heat, we were plenty warm enough, but the occasional nip of cold added to the urgent thrill of what we were doing.

He started moving his tongue in swirling circles around the round bulge of my tip, tasting every bit of it he could as he slowly took more of me in. He worked his way up the trunk of my cock until he had half of it resting on his tongue, then he slid back out and down again. I felt the warmth swelling within me urging me onward. My balls were heavy. Herding a bunch of people around with Connor had made me admire him as much as I enjoyed laughing with him. It made me crave him all the more. I didn't meet many people who resonated with me like he did.

As much as I wanted him to swallow what I had to give him right then and there, I had other plans for tonight. I hadn't been lying when I told Connor I had something in mind. Connor was dragging his tongue along the bottom of my cock when I squeezed his hair and pulled him slowly off me.

I reached inside my jacket pockets and took out a small bottle of lube and a condom, and I gave Connor a sharp nod.

"Pants off. Completely," I ordered him.

Connor didn't hesitate. The chill outside only seemed to spur him on as he tore his boots and pants off while I put on the condom and lube. The moment he was exposed before me, I reached down and hoisted him up by the hips. He slid his legs around my hips, and I held him under the ass as I spread his cheeks and slid the tip of my cock against his hole.

"I can't believe I'm doing this," Connor breathed, fastening his hands around the back of my neck. "I—fuck, don't get me wrong, you're incredible. But I'd never thought of myself as the kind of person who'd—"

"Who'd shut up and learn his place when I'm taking what I want from him?" I snarled, and the blush that came over Connor's face was as red as my flannel.

"Yes, sir," he complied, and I began teasing his hole with the tip of my cock.

I started slowly, pushing its way around and exploring the tightness that Connor held against me. He groaned as I started to work my way in, and little by little, he welcomed me. His body knew it loved my presence, and it wanted to serve me as much as I craved.

His back pounded against the wall as I thrust a little further into him, and once I felt those pulsing waves of delicious pleasure rolling up my body as the hole surrounded my cock, Connor was in my complete control. He tried to squirm and use his grip to keep up with me, and he most definitely enhanced the feeling rolling through me, but it was my iron grip that held him up and let him do that.

He loved that as much as it annoyed him, I thought. He tried to struggle for dominance now and then when I was thrusting into him, but he could never quite make me match his pace. I was the one calling the shots, and even though we kept our voices silent to avoid drawing attention, we were battling back and forth as much as we were fucking.

I loved it. He squirmed under my authority in bed. He tested me. I pushed back. As I felt a burst of precome escape me while my cock ground against him deep within, I knew we sharpened each other the way only two skilled people could.

At last, I couldn't hold back any longer, and I didn't want to. I let myself come, and I groaned as I shot my hot, pearly release with every thrust. I nodded, and Connor reached down with one of his hands to grab his own cock and let himself burst almost immediately. I leaned forward and kissed him to keep him from groaning loudly, and up against the wall together, we were a pulsing mess of heat and sweat before the rush finally slowed down, and I slowly disentangled us.

I panted as I leaned against the wall and watched Connor pull his pants back on, blushing furiously and smiling up at me.

"Do you think they've missed us yet?" Connor asked.

"If they did," I said, chuckling, "they can wait. Let's go get cleaned up."

9

CONNOR

I WOKE TO THE WARMTH OF THE SUN ON MY FACE AND SMILED. Underneath the covers, I was warm and cozy, like I was wrapped up in a cocoon. Everything around me was soft and warm, and I felt strangely… safe. Like no harm could possibly come to me as long as I was tucked neatly away in this bed.

It reminded me of winter mornings back home, when I would wake up to feel a slight chill, unusual for where I come from around LA. I would lie there, marveling at how comfortable I was despite the cool temperature. I was always an energetic kid, so I tended to need less sleep than my family members. I would always wake up early, usually before the sun had even finished its ascent into the sky, and just lie there in the peace and quiet.

Even back then, as a child, I was deeply contemplative. I would take those early morning silent hours to just think. Daydream deeply. Whisk myself away on some blustery wind of my own imagination, carrying me off to an adventure in an exotic land or alternate reality. I would look up at the popcorn ceiling and find faint faces and shapes in the mottled material's shadows and peaks, almost like someone might derive a constellation or imagine the clouds into shapes. It was the calm before the storm, an opportunity for me to relax and ground myself. I explored all sorts of philosophical queries I put upon myself, thinking my way through complicated feelings and experiences just by calmly navigating through my daydreams. By the time everyone else in my family had woken up at a more appropriate hour, I had already been on several adventures in my head. It didn't occur to me until much later, as an adult, that those early mornings spent imagining faraway places were a form of meditation.

No wonder I made such good grades in school—I was cerebrally wide awake long before the first bell rang for class. I wrote stories and poems in my diary. I recorded bits and pieces of my dreams, almost like a scientist objectively recording information from an experiment. I was never bored, because even when the world around me was dull and monotonous—following my class schedule, hearing my classmates' chatter on and on about gossip I couldn't care less about—it was never dull inside my brain. There were always new worlds to discover. New, exciting people to meet. Sometimes my teachers would remark to my parents about how I seemed to have my head in the clouds, but they could never really argue about it because I still made good grades. It wasn't that I was trying to be difficult or disrespectful, I just needed more stimulation and excitement than I was ever going to eke out of learning long division.

And could you really blame me? The choice between doing math and dreaming about an Arctic expedition complete with polar bears and narwhals was an easy one. Dreams over arithmetic, every time. I would learn the long division, too, but I definitely didn't look like I was paying enough attention to do it correctly. Still, the grades stayed good and my imagination only became more and more vivid over time. Sometimes, my thoughts could even get away from me, taking me on some wild goose chase for no reason.

Even today, I could easily get lost in my own thoughts, let them climb and swarm around me, keeping me in a lulled state of self-amusement. It was hard to be bored when there was always a party happening in my head. Right now was no exception. I lay there in the peace and quiet, just listening to the soft rhythmic inhales and exhales of the gorgeous man beside me. Grayson was still asleep, his lips slightly parted and his eyes gently fluttering behind his eyelids, like he was dreaming viscerally about something. I stared at his handsome face and wondered where he went in moments like this. Where did he go? What or who was he dreaming about? Was it me? Did I dare to believe it ever could be someone like me?

Was that just narcissistic of me, to want him to dream about me? After all, I had certainly had my fair share of dreams involving him. I closed my eyes and thought about the greatest hits so far. Some of them were fairly innocent—the two of us tromping through the mystical, foggy woods of evergreens, the last dregs of snowfall crunching with the dead leaves under our boots. We could climb and climb higher up the slope of the picturesque green mountain-side until we arrived at a magical brook with the clearest water one could ever imagine. Every ripple of the water sounded like the low trill of a woodland fairy, singing lullabies to her daisy-petal children.

Some of the dreams were like that: sweet and romantic. But other dreams of Grayson were more… intense. The two of us locked in an elevator together, the box hanging idly in the shaft while things heated up. We would kiss and grope and rut against one another until we couldn't take it anymore. With the delicious cocktail of sweat, desire, and arousal in the air, Grayson would pick me up and pin me against the metal wall. My legs would wrap around his waist as we began to move together, grunting and groaning with pleasure. I belonged to him and he belonged to me, and…

I opened my eyes again. This time, things were different. I noticed that the world was no longer dead-still. There was movement under the layers of blankets. I turned to see that Grayson's beautiful, piercing eyes were just starting to flutter open. His hair was all tousled and he had some stubble that made him look even sexier than before, somehow.

"G'morning," I murmured.

"Morning," he grunted roughly.

"Well, I should probably get up and start the day," I sighed, turning away to slide out of bed.

But before I could even get one leg out from under the blankets, a strong, muscular arm hooked around me and gently pulled me back.

"Oh no, you don't," Grayson whispered. "Not going to let you go that easily."

I smiled languidly, allowing him to pull me close to his chest, my back facing him. He rutted against me slowly, lazily, like we had all the time in the world. And in this moment, we kind of did. It was early. I had a feeling none of my colleagues were up yet. I might as well make the most of a lie-in, so I began to roll my hips subtly. I pressed my taut ass back up against Grayson's crotch, moaning as I felt him getting harder and stiffer for me. It was exhilarating to know I was the one responsible for his pleasure, for his satisfaction. And when he reached an arm over my body to start stroking my cock through the thin fabric of my pajama pants, I shivered with anticipation. It felt so fucking good—his hand lightly massaging my cock while I pressed back into him. We were rocking and swaying now, taking our time, gathering pleasure and building the tension ever higher, all without taking our clothes off.

"Turn around for me," Grayson growled in my ear, sending shivers down my spine.

I felt tingly and hot all over, my arousal growing every second. I did as I was told, slowly rotating in bed so that I was facing Grayson. I nearly lost my breath as I looked squarely into his eyes. There was a fire burning there, and I was instantly fascinated by the slope of his nose, the hard, chiseled appearance of his cheekbones, the fullness of his lips. Those dark brows were ever so slightly furrowed in a way that made him look both sexy and pensive. I wriggled closer to him and he leaned in to kiss me. Warmth rolled down my body as I sank into his heat, his touch. Grayson wrapped his arms around me and pulled me in tight, his cock pressing harder against my thigh, while my cock pressed against his. There were a couple layers of thin fabric between us, but it might as well have been nothing. In fact, the added barrier kind of added more stimulation to our little game. We kissed and nipped at each other's lips, our hands roving and exploring each other's bodies while our cocks slid up and down, back and forth together. We were both moaning and gasping now, feeling the tension increase to a fever pitch as finally, with a few more frantic rolls of the hips, we both came together, spurting seed down the front of our pajama pants as we held each other. We breathed slowly and sighed through the shared orgasm. I knew my face had to be bright pink, but to his credit, Grayson didn't tease me for it. Instead, he gently kissed my forehead and took my hand, giving it a little tug.

"Come on. Let's get cleaned up," he murmured.

"Whatever you say," I replied, staring up at him with pure adoration.

He smiled and led me to the bathroom, where we changed out of our, uh, wet clothes and slipped into the warm, steamy rain shower. We held each other under the hot spray, enjoying the sensation of our sweat and sleep washing away down the drain. We took our time there, shampooing and conditioning each other's hair, lathering up one another's bodies. It was so sweet and strangely domestic, something I never expected to do with a guy like Grayson. But if there was one thing I could say about him for sure, it was that he was full of surprises.

After our shower, we put on big fluffy robes and warm slippers. We padded out onto the en suite balcony to gaze out over the beautiful white expanse. The snowbank had to be around seven or eight feet by now, and in the morning sun it glittered and sparkled like a sea of sequins. The sky above was clear and sunny, and I found myself unable to wipe the smile off my face as I stood there on the deck, looking at the mystical, almost alien world around us while the most magical man I'd ever met stood beside me. In this moment, I felt no anxiety. No rush. No panic. I had no urge to be anywhere else in the world but right here. For once, my daydreams had met their match. This reality was the softest and most comfortable reality yet. And it was real.

"It's beautiful today, isn't it?" I said softly.

"At least the sun is shining. That's a good sign," Grayson replied.

I looked over at him quizzically. "A good sign of what?" I asked.

"That the snow will start melting faster," he answered simply.

"That sun will shrink down the snow banks. It will be a little slushy out there for a while, but after that, it'll clear out so that you won't be trapped here anymore. With me."

For the first time all morning, a little flicker of anxiety licked through my insides. My heart sank. I knew he was right, and it was painful to imagine. I realized bitterly that I didn't want the snow to melt. Well, I did. I wanted it to melt so that we might get some of the outdoor shoots our team had planned for. But I also didn't want it to melt, because that would spell the end for my subarctic tryst with Grayson. I had gotten pretty used to waking up next to him already, and the idea of not being trapped in a place with him in close quarters was painful to think about. I never wanted him out of my sight. I wanted to be with him all the time, or at least to feel safe in the knowledge that he was nearby if I needed him, if I wanted him.

And god, did I ever want him.

I loved the way he held me, the way he kissed me, the way he pushed me to think creatively and be my best version of myself. Beyond that, I actually enjoyed feeling like I had someone to belong to. Someone more than worthy of possessing me. Out here, we were so isolated. Sure, there were the photographers and the models and the skeleton crew at the lodge, but in moments like this one it was easy enough to push all that out of my mind and just imagine that we were alone here, just Grayson and me. That was the greatest reality, the ultimate daydream. Anywhere I could be alone with Grayson was what I wanted. But all good things had to come to an end, right? I needed to start preparing myself for the reality of leaving this place behind, flying back to Anchorage to start the next leg of my career. But then, I remembered with a flutter of my heart, that Grayson was also based in Anchorage. We would be close. Maybe there was the faintest, slimmest chance we could keep this up on some level. I still wasn't sure how he really felt about the things we did together. I mean, he certainly seemed to enjoy it, but was that enough? Was I enough for him?

He broke me out of my deep thoughts by clearing his throat. I looked at him, blinking as I came back to the present moment. "Oh. Sorry. I guess I zoned out a little there," I apologized.

Grayson smiled softly. "No worries. But I have an idea."

"Oh? What is it?" I asked, turning to face him as I leaned my elbow on the balcony rail.

"I think a big, communal breakfast would be fantastic for morale, don't you?" he suggested, the cogs already turning in his handsome head.

"That's a great idea," I said excitedly.

"It's settled then. Let's go," he said, taking me by the hand. Again, my heart leapt.

We headed down the vaulted hall to the coffee bar and began prep for a gigantic breakfast feast. We had a lot of people to feed, all with varying degrees of pickiness and dietary neuroses—it came with the territory of working with models. I didn't blame them for being calorie—or macro—obsessed. The industry certainly did not reward anyone who didn't adhere to the damn near impossible standard of beauty and fitness required of them.

But that didn't stop Grayson. He wasn't going to give them a grapefruit and black coffee—oh no. Coffee was definitely happening, no doubt about that. We were all a bunch of caffeine addicts here, and sure enough, all it took was a whiff of that freshly-brewed espresso smell to waft through the lodge and other people started emerging like little sea turtles out of the sand.

Everyone looked a little sleepy and sore from all the shoots and workouts, but they seemed happy. There were smiles all around, and when Landon came in and decided to jump on stove duty, the air was filled with the delicious scents of sizzling bacon, a heap of scrambled eggs, and a stack of buttered toast high enough to rival the Tower of Babel. Some of the stricter dieters chopped up fruit and made smoothies to compliment the more calorie-rich options. More and more people showed up to help, and before long, there was an assembly line of cooks, sous chefs, and clean-up partners in the cafe. Everyone was laughing and chatting, having a great time as we bonded over that most universal of indulgences: food.

But there was something biting at me, something I couldn't quite shake. It took me a few minutes to determine what it was: jealousy. Insecurity. It hit me that Grayson was quite literally surrounded by beautiful, physically-flawless models right now… and then there was me. I was a good-looking guy, and I was aware of it, but even I knew better than to try and compete with people whose entire livelihood depended on how hot they were. And it didn't help that I got the sense a few of my models might have a little bit of a crush on Grayson. Again, I couldn't exactly blame them for that. After all, I was nursing a big, fat infatuation for the guy myself. He was irresistible and charismatic, a natural-born leader to whom people just seemed to gravitate. He always had a clever idea up his sleeve, and he knew how to turn any negative into a positive.

That kind of power and influence was intoxicating to be around, and I knew some of my models were already being sucked into the Grayson spiral. It wasn't that I felt threatened by the models, just that I hoped it wasn't a problem for Grayson that I didn't quite look like them. If by chance they were more his type, I would have to just deal with it. I couldn't make someone want me.

However, my fears were assuaged when suddenly Grayson came walking over to drape his strong, thick arms over my shoulders as he showed me the most efficient way to chop an avocado to top off the eggs and toast. He murmured instructions and tips in my ear, giving me goosebumps of pleasure. He was paying attention to me and me alone, and I was living for it. Even as he took special requests and whipped up some seriously complicated and delicious coffee drinks for the models, he always returned to stay close by me. I felt so warm and fuzzy and giddy inside, it was a feeling I wanted to capture in a bottle and keep forever.

I knew it was all temporary, but man, I really didn't want this to ever end.

10

GRAYSON

LATER THAT AFTERNOON, I WAS IN THE BATHROOM OF MY OWN SUITE, finishing a quick shave and washing the last of the shaving cream off my face in the hot sink water. I felt the smooth surface of my face and decided I was satisfied, then used a towel to dab myself dry before looking myself over in the mirror and leaving the bathroom.

I slid a simple black tank top over my shoulders, and I was wearing a pair of iron gray gym shorts that hugged my ass just enough to let me know I'd be bothering Connor next time I walked by him. I had to smile to myself as I caught a glimpse in the mirror on my way out, and I chuckled, shaking my head.

I was not the kind of man who spent a lot of time worrying about his appearance, but I'd taken a little extra care to clean myself up today. I was so used to flying from place to place with the cold cabin air keeping me company that a fresh shave and face scrub was a lot rarer than the usual quick shower before bolting off to the next job.

If we were trapped somewhere fancy, I might as well look the part, I figured, but even that made me laugh to myself as I made my way downstairs. The idea that anything could make me look like something approaching pampered was far-fetched. Then again, I was among other men who certainly took care of the way they looked.

Speaking of the models, three of them were sitting in the lounge at the bottom of the stairs, not far from one of the bars where one of them appeared to be trying to make a cocktail.

Erik, Andrew, and Tomas were in the middle of a discussion about workout routines their various trainers over the years had put them through, the perks and downsides to the different styles, and using a lot of names and terms I didn't recognize. It was strange to walk in on a conversation about something I should have thought was second nature to me, but by the way they talked, I didn't know the first thing about exercise.

Well, my results spoke for themselves.

Andrew, the lone American among the models, was the first to notice me coming down and gave a nod. "Hey, Grayson. We were just talking about you."

"Everything you've heard is slander," I grunted as I reached the bottom of the stairs, and they chuckled.

"Sure hope not," Andrew said with a gruff smile as I approached the group and crossed my arms. "Because we were just wondering how you got that figure on your own up here. I know guys who have professional trainers who don't look as cut as you."

His tone told me it was a perfectly innocent comment—like the rest of the models, Andrew hadn't once looked at me the way Connor did, and I didn't see any of them that way either.

"Me?" I asked, raising an eyebrow. "I'm not the one posing for shots."

"Yeah, and you made me jealous, so fess up," Erik said with a friendly smile, clearly teasing.

I scratched the back of my head, honestly trying to think of what to tell the guy. My workout routine wasn't something I put a lot of thought into—it just came naturally with what I did for a living, plus genetics.

"Well, I spend most of my time moving cargo by hand around places commercial airlines are too scared to go," I said while Erik at the bar started pouring a double-shot of whiskey without being asked and sliding it in my general direction. "And when I'm not doing that, I keep up my home back in Anchorage on my own—yardwork, landscaping, basic homeowner maintenance, that kind of thing."

The models bobbed their heads, Erik and Tomas obviously having absolutely no frame of reference for what I was talking about. Andrew, on the other hand, seemed to be following along with interest.

"So, just your lifestyle?" Andrew asked. "That's it?"

"That's not *it*," I admitted. "I eat well up here. High protein. Fresh food."

"You mean... not everything is canned or frozen up here?" Erik asked.

"It is if you want to eat like you do down in California," I said, approaching the bar and taking the whiskey glass with a subtle nod. "Cold weather crops grow well here. You eat that, you're eating healthy. And we're always moving, always burning calories. The faint of heart move south."

I wasn't talking as if I was bragging—life could be hard up here, and I meant it when I said it wasn't for the faint of heart. Andrew, on the other hand, looked pensive.

"Guess when you put it that way, you can really keep your body in shape when you're not tied up in meetings with agents all the time," Andrew remarked, almost more to himself than to the group as he scratched his chin in thought. "Huh."

At that moment, Connor appeared from the other end of the kitchen, making his way toward the adjacent lounge wearing a sharp button-down that was rolled up to the sleeves. He wore the kind of smile on his face that told me he'd been busy getting some undoubtedly impressive work done handling the other models. I gave him a warm smile and raised my glass to him as he approached.

"But if you're in his hands," I said to the others, nodding to Connor, "you don't have anything to worry about."

"Wait, who's in my hands now?" he asked, glancing around at the group as I smiled and offered him a drink of whiskey from my glass in front of the others.

Out of the corner of my eye, I saw Erik and Tomas share the

briefest knowing glance, but Connor's eyes had flitted to Andrew. I hoped he didn't worry that there was any chemistry between the two of us. That had barely crossed my mind. We were here in a romantic lodge full of some of the most beautiful men from all around the world, and I hadn't even given them so much as a glance in the same way I wanted Connor.

It was a ridiculous thought I wouldn't have even had if I hadn't noticed the slightest twinge in Connor's face. I'd have to do something about that, I decided. Good thing I already had plans for the evening that would suit that purpose perfectly.

"Grayson was just telling us about how he keeps himself in shape like that," Andrew said with a grin.

"And bragging on you," Erik added with a smirk.

"I was actually just looking for you," I said to Connor before tossing back the rest of the whiskey and setting it on the table. I glanced at the others. "We can talk about pilot work another time. Thanks for the drink."

Smiling ominously down at Connor, I nodded toward the gym and started heading in that direction with him at my side.

"I've got to say, I'm relieved they don't drive you nuts," Connor said in a low tone. "I get along with most of them, but I always assumed it would just be a conflict of personality."

"They're alright," I said with a soft chuckle. "Careful though, I get the impression Andrew might be craving something outside the modeling life."

"Oh god," Connor said, his expression still lighthearted. "I mean, that's fine if it's true, I just hope he doesn't tell our journalist that this week was so inspiring he decided to quit."

I snorted a laugh and slipped my hand up behind his neck as we walked, giving it a gentle, massaging squeeze before running it down to scratch his back affectionately.

"I don't think he meant it like that," I assured him as I held the door to the gym open for him. "But anyway, that's not what I wanted to get you in private to talk about. I had something else in mind entirely."

"If you wanted to do a private workout session, you could have just asked," Connor said as we crossed the gymnasium, and I watched our tall figures in the wall of mirrors on the far end of the facility.

"Something like that," I said.

"Should I stop and go get changed?" he asked, slowing down and jabbing a thumb in the direction of the gym's small locker room.

I slowed down too, but only to smile, take Connor by the scruff of his collar, and guide him along with me toward one of the side-rooms I had located.

"Don't need to," I informed him as I brought him inside, and I let him take in the sight.

It was a room probably meant for private workouts. About five people could comfortably stand in the square room with one wall lined with mirrors. I turned the dial on the light switch to give us dim lighting, and when I closed the door behind us, we were sealed off from the rest of the lodge, even more so when I turned the lock and clicked the door shut. Connor noticed that, and he was starting to catch on when he saw me lock the door behind us.

"A *very* private workout session?" he asked with a playful smile. "You know I should be keeping an eye on the models right now."

"I want your eyes on me," I said simply but firmly, approaching him. "You've worked hard, but I want you to work harder for me."

I nodded to the center of the room, where Connor saw what I had in store for him.

I had dragged a bench from one of the pieces of exercise equipment into this side room. On it was draped a thick pile of black rope I'd found in the gym's storage room, presumably intended for some kind of workout or exercise equipment. They looked like the kinds of cords that would be able to support some weight, but flexible enough to work with. Next to that was a single, simple black handkerchief of my own.

"*...oh,*" said Connor.

I rested a heavy hand on his shoulder and smiled, then led him forward like an executioner at the gallows. "I had an idea, Connor.

Something I've been wanting to try with the right person, and it just so happens, this place provides."

"This is definitely what I think it is, then," he said, reaching down and stroking his fingers over the ropes.

I stripped my shirt off and tossed it aside, then started to unbutton his one by one, glaring down at him as if he were my prey. "Only if you're willing to submit," I growled. "You have to be ready for this. If you don't want it, or if you're hesitant, this stops."

He licked his lips.

"You know I know the safe word," he said, raising his eyebrows in challenge at me. "If I need it, I'll use it."

I felt the fire in my chest swell, and I gripped his shirt and ripped the remaining buttons off, sending them clattering across the floor. If he was going to push me like that, he'd face the consequences. I spun him around and reached around to grab his belt and pull it off in one swift motion. Immediately, I pulled his wrists behind his back and tied his wrists together. It would serve in the short term.

With his hands secured, I reached for the handkerchief and folded it into a blindfold to wrap around his eyes. It almost felt like a kidnapping. Once that was tied, I gripped his pants and slid them down slowly. When I saw how stiff his cock was when it bobbed out, I murmured in approval before helping him step out of his pants.

"Down," I commanded as I guided him to straddle the bench.

"Are you going to gag me, too?" he asked, a blatant challenge.

I responded by cracking a hand across his ass sharply and forcing him down to the padded bench, pressing his face against it gently but firmly.

"No," I snarled. "I've got something else to fill it with."

He shivered before I slid back and grabbed the ropes.

Kneeling behind Connor and gazing at the ass I was about to claim, I carefully wrapped the ropes around Connor's arms, binding his wrists together in a firm, snug grip that showed him how tight a leash I could keep him on. But I wasn't done there. I brought the loose ends of the rope down along either side of Connor's hips and thighs, and I bound his legs together at the ankle.

"Now," I said once I finished the intricate knots, "squirm for me."

He obeyed, and his breathing got faster when he realized the ropes couldn't quite let him stand up from his position. He was truly trapped and bent forward, and he bit his lip, blushing furiously.

"You uh... damn," he murmured. "You know your way around some knots, don't you? What kind of things do you get up to in Kenai?"

"Not this, unfortunately," I growled, "but I've helped string up game before. Does that count?" I growled, squatting down and saying it right into his ear.

As I stood up, I took hold of his hair and guided his mouth to my cock.

"You're going to feel what it's like to have me in complete command," I said. "Now, open."

Connor sheepishly opened his mouth, and I slid my cock into him. He closed his mouth around my bulging crown and moaned as he pressed his tongue into it. He didn't hold back, I felt his wet, hot tongue caress my mass and give it all the attention it craved. It was like he could sense my body and know just where to touch me to make me hunger for more.

My will told him how fast he could work. I held his hair, and if I didn't want him to move forward yet, I'd hold him there. He fought me sometimes, and I felt a thrill run up my spine like electricity each time.

I finally slid him the rest of the way onto my cock, taking him by surprise, but he didn't choke. He adapted, and I soon felt waves of heat rolling up my shaft and through my entire groin. His tongue was sliding up and down my cock, from the base of the trunk to the edge of the crown, as much as he could squirm his head around in my grip. A tight leash was putting it lightly.

"That's it," I growled. "Serve me. I'm giving you the release you need, and you need to thank me. You deserve it."

He moaned in affirmative, and I felt a nod before I slid him slowly off my cock and looked at his blindfolded face and the hungry mouth still hanging open. I gave a single, ominous chuckle and slowly walked around to his backside, where I groped his ass with a thoughtful rumble.

"I like the way you feel," I said. "If this is what you're going to give up to me… I'll consider it."

"You drive a hard bargain," he breathed.

I spanked him once more before I reached under the bench, where I had stored lubricant and a condom to use. I put both on, and without warning, I stuck two fingers into Connor's mouth like a fish hook, listening to him yelp while I wetted my fingers. When I brought the hand back, I lowered it to the ass I spread with the other hand.

He drew in a sharp breath as I slid a finger into him and swirled it around, not holding back or being gentle with him as I felt his body up. He was such a hardworking man that I knew the stress relief I was giving him was worth every second of the act, but it meant so much more than that to me that he'd trust me with this whole spectacle.

It set him apart, in my eyes.

Another finger joined the first. "I'm going to claim you now, Connor," I growled. "The way I wanted to the second you set foot on my plane."

"I want to feel you try," he hissed, and my heart tried to pound out of its cage.

I seized Connor's hips and pulled them up to slide my cock against his hole, and I pushed into him slowly. Just as he groaned, I pulled back and went in once more, each thrust taking me slowly into him. Despite the rough tone I spoke to him with and the way I thrust his body around so easily, my cock fit so perfectly in his ass that it couldn't be anything but bliss for both of us.

Connor faced the mirror, and I could see his mouth hanging open, cheeks blushing, and he pushed his face against the bench's surface to moan in delight as I sank further into him. He tried his restraints, truly—I heard the fibers groan under the pressure he could exert. He was a strong man, but my ropes were stronger.

I could tame him.

And every time my cock ground against his insides, I proved that I already had.

"More," I growled, thrusting harder. "I want more from you."

"Everything," he breathed. "I can't move. I can't see. God, all I can feel is you in me!"

"Good," I snarled. "You're better off."

Our rutting grew more and more fierce, and as I groped and pinched his ass with each thrust, I finally felt the pressure grow too strong to ignore. All at once, a chorus of feelings swelled up and made every nerve stand on end to get skimmed by white-hot fire I felt spreading from my cock all the way up to my nipples, electrifying me and paralyzing me as I came inside him. A sharp breath from Connor told me he was coming with me, without even needing to be commanded to. I held the ropes between his wrists and his ankles as our orgasms shook us with every fast, hard pump.

And when it ended, I stared at our glistening, panting reflections in the mirrors before reaching forward and slipping Connor's blindfold off. He blushed at the sight of us, and I felt him shiver and pulse with a soft groan.

"You've done well," I growled, stroking him and bending down to kiss him with every rope I took off. "Very well."

"Mmph," Connor said in response, looking so peaceful and overjoyed he could have been an angel—an exhausted angel.

I chuckled as I kissed him and cuddled against him as I helped him out of his bindings, and once it was done, I helped him to his feet slowly.

"But let's not hang out much longer," I grunted. "We've got some cleanup to do before someone comes looking for us."

11

CONNOR

ONE THING I WAS LEARNING ABOUT THIS LODGE WAS THAT THERE seemed to be an almost endless number of sitting rooms and study nooks full of plush, antique, well-made furniture to sink into and get comfortable while working. Back home, I had this favorite cafe I used to visit several times a week. I would get there early, right after they opened, post up comfortably at a corner table by the window, and get to work while I sipped my favorite cinnamon latte. I liked being by the window so that I could people-watch, which was one of the best forms of procrastination I had discovered thus far. I would take breaks from my work to just watch families slowly herding their wild-haired toddlers down the sidewalk, young couples blushing and getting all sweaty as they held hands for perhaps the first time ever. There were businessmen with their no-nonsense haircuts and their clean-shaven faces, carrying leathery briefcases and almost always arguing with someone through an earpiece.

Tonight, though, I was in a different kind of space. There were no passersby to subtly gawk at and come up with backgrounds for. It was just me, alone, curled over a laptop in one of the opulent sitting rooms of the lodge. The chair was made of plush, dark green velvet, and the writing desk I was using seemed to be an antique. The woodgrain was intricate and almost mesmerizing to the eye. I had a steamy mug of spiked coffee just the way I liked it sitting on the desk on a coaster, and through the big bay window in front of me I could see the wintry landscape beyond the confines of the building.

I was working, going through and methodically responding to every single one of the myriad messages and questions in my email. Even though we all had a pretty solid thing going on here at the lodge, my investors and superiors still wanted me to give them regular check-ins and stay in communication. I had a lot to catch up on, but at least I got to do my work in this beautiful, cozy setting.

As I fired off another email, my eyes were distracted by the ethereal plume of curling steam wafting from my coffee mug. It looked like some kind of tiny spirit, twisting and dancing in the split seconds before the cool air could swallow it up into nothing. I sighed and took another sip, wishing I could have made my drink—and my evening—just a pinch more exciting by adding an additional shot. It already had a single shot of Irish cream in it, and it was delicious without a doubt, but I was craving something a little stronger. I wanted to indulge a little, make the most of every second I got to spend in this luxurious, beautiful environment. This place had proven to be pretty damn conducive to creativity so far, and I felt lucky to have had everything fall into place so perfectly. Of course, none of my success here would have been possible without the priceless help and guidance of Grayson. He was the mastermind. He was the genius. And he was the hero who saved us all, first from the snow, second from burnout.

After sending off the last of my emails, for the time being, I leaned back in the cozy armchair and sipped my coffee, staring out over the landscape. The trees were barely-visible shadows arching up into the early evening sky, which was streaked with grayish gold and lilac. Everything seemed to glitter and glow from within, like Alaska was just thrumming with some primordial magic few mortals would ever fully understand. This place was full of mystery, and it made perfect sense to me that growing up here would foster some truly mysterious, intriguing individuals. It didn't take a rocket scientist to figure out who exactly I was thinking about.

And then, almost as though he was taking a cue from my internal thoughts somehow, Grayson came sauntering into the sitting room, looking every bit as rugged and handsome as he always did. My breath caught in my throat and my face burned, my whole body tingly and giddy at the sight of him. That was all it took. One look in his direction and I was putty in his hands. He had a look on his face that made my heart skip a beat.

"Well, hello there," I said, hoping I didn't sound silly.

"How's it going? You're just hiding in here," he teased, walking over to stand next to my chair. He laid a heavy hand on my shoulder and I trembled at his touch. God, he had such a hold over me. It was almost criminal.

"Had a lot of work to catch up on," I sighed.

"Anything exciting?" he prompted.

I snorted and shook my head. "Not unless you consider answering business emails to be exciting," I remarked.

He wrinkled his nose. "Mm, no. Not so much. But I suppose somebody's got to do it."

"You can say that again. I swear the creative portion of my job is so tiny compared to the administrative parts. I spend so much time going through and answering emails, sometimes I feel like my vision will go cross-eyed if I stare at my computer screen for another minute," I said.

Grayson reached down and delicately took my chin in his hand, smirking down at me. I froze up, not even daring to breathe as he traced his thumb over my bottom lip. He licked his own lips, making my cock stir between my legs. Really? That was all it took?

"I think you've done enough busy work for the moment," he said in a low growl. "You said it yourself, you might go cross-eyed if you don't take a break."

I chuckled softly, remembering to breathe again. "I was only joking," I mumbled.

He leaned down and cupped my face, those eyes blazing as they gazed into mine.

"I wasn't," he hissed. "Come on. Shut that damn laptop and come take a break with me. You've earned it. Besides, there's something upstairs I've been dying to show you. No buts. Well, except for yours."

"Ha-ha," I said, even as I couldn't help but grin. "You got me. I'm at the mercy of your whims. Take me away, maestro."

He quirked an eyebrow at my silly remark but to his credit, it didn't faze him.

"Come on. Follow me," he instructed.

I could only do as I was told. Besides, the last time he had something to show me, it was definitely worth it, so I dutifully followed him upstairs and down a winding hallway. This place was absolutely gigantic and almost labyrinthine with all its passageways and hideaway nooks. It almost seemed to grow bigger and more fantastic as the days wore on. Just like Grayson, there was always something new to discover. But when we walked into our destination, my eyes widened, and my jaw dropped. It was incredible. We were in a sumptuous room, the walls covered with glossy window panes that showed off the beauty of the wilderness outside, the night sky in all its mystical glory. There was a Jacuzzi in the middle of the room large enough to fit a whole party, but the best part of the whole setup wasn't evident at first glance.

With a wry, knowing smile on his lips, Grayson walked over and took my hand. He leaned in close to my ear and whispered, "Look up at the ceiling, Connor."

I was a little confused by the command, but I trusted him. I looked up to find that there was a massive skylight allowing the moonlight to spill through. I gasped and felt tears of joy stinging in my eyes as I slowly realized what Grayson was trying to show me.

The northern lights. I could see them turning in hues of evanescent green, purple, white—like three gigantic angels spinning in a slow dance across the night sky.

"Oh my god," I murmured breathlessly, staring up with complete awe.

"I know. It's beautiful, isn't it? Have you ever seen it before?" he asked softly.

I shook my head, never tearing my eyes away from the magical lights in the sky.

"No. Well, yes, but only in photos. This is a first for me, Grayson. This is incredible," I gushed openly. "I never imagined I would be lucky enough to see something like this."

"Well, consider yourself welcomed into the fold by Alaska herself," Grayson said. "Looks like this land is willing to make you one of her own, after all. This is a rite of passage, Connor, but not everyone is so lucky."

"I can't believe this. Sometimes I wonder if I must be stuck in a dream," I sighed.

Without warning, Grayson stepped closer to me and pulled me close to him, pressing a soft but passionate kiss against my lips. I sighed into the kiss, melting into his embrace. His strong arms draped around me, almost cradling me like I was something precious, something to be jealously guarded. Grayson touched me like I belonged to him and I was his to protect, and to be perfectly honest, I loved it. I felt secure in the knowledge that he possessed me, that I had finally found a man to whom I could relinquish all control. I knew he would never lead me astray. He kept me safe and happy. He kept my imagination stimulated and my body warm and happy. Grayson was like a guardian angel put on earth, and I couldn't believe my good fortune to have found him. It was so serendipitous that it felt like only fate could have led us here to this moment, clutching one another and swaying gently side to side under the dancing northern lights.

When he broke our kiss, there was a dark desire brewing behind those gorgeous eyes and I held my breath, awaiting instruction. I was his. I would do as he said, now and always.

"Strip for me," he hissed, sending chills down my spine. "I want to see you. All of you."

I bit my lip and took a half step back, starting to slowly lift up my shirt. Grayson stared openly and unabashedly at me, a little half-smile on his handsome face. He looked hungry for me, like he was a wild wolf poised to lunge and devour me at any moment. It was hot as hell. I took my time stripping off my clothes for him, not turning it into a show, but certainly milking it for all it was worth. And boy was it worth the trouble, getting to see the lust slowly grow on Grayson's handsome face. He groaned his approval once I was fully nude in front of him.

"You're fantastic, you know that?" he growled as he stepped closer to me.

I could feel waves of desire rolling off of him. It was almost dizzying.

"Well, what about you? You must have some seriously crazy stamina to want me after all the… uh, activities we have been doing together," I said, just a little cheekily.

He brushed off the compliment easily. "I'm a physically active guy, what can I say?" he replied, his hands starting to rove up and down my body, feeling me up.

He gripped my waist, then my thighs, my taut ass. He lightly stroked my cock as it stirred to life, just gently teasing me and making me even harder for him.

"I like to be in control, in and out of the bedroom," Grayson purred as he reached to stroke my face. I leaned into his palm, closing my eyes with contentment. "You needed a break, and I am the one who's going to give it to you. So for the time being, you are going to forget all about your responsibilities, your obligations. Right now, your only obligation is to yourself. And to me."

"Happy and willing," I breathed as his hands smoothed down my biceps and forearms.

"Good. Keep watching those lights. Relax. Let loose, Connor," he commanded softly.

He took me by the hand and led me slowly to the Jacuzzi. I could feel the tempting steam rising up out of the bubbly water, and my attention to the northern lights split for a moment as I greedily watched Grayson strip out of his clothes, too. We were standing stark naked now, and we slid into the big, toasty Jacuzzi together, each sighing with delight.

"It's been years since I was in a Jacuzzi," I said, tilting my head back as I got comfortable, so I could keep watching the northern lights.

"Sounds like you were overdue for this then," Grayson murmured.

He pulled me closer and pressed a kiss against my cheek, making me blush. His hand found mine under the hot, bubbling water and he interlaced his fingers with mine. We sat there in comfortable, relaxing silence for a few minutes, just enjoying the comforting hot water and the magical light show up in the sky.

I looked at Grayson with amusement. "You know, the models are downstairs right now making hot cocoa and swapping scary stories," I chuckled.

"What? Like they're all at sleepaway camp?" he scoffed, entertained by the idea.

"Yeah, they're going up to one of those fire pit things on the roof with a bunch of blankets. I'm sure they just want a better vantage point to see the lights," I explained.

"Would you rather be there?" Grayson asked.

I was so stunned by the absurdity of his question I almost started coughing.

"Oh my god, no," I said, a little more fiercely than I intended. I went on in a more casual tone. "I just mean to say that as much fun as they're probably having, there is nowhere else in the world I would rather be right now."

"Well, in that case, maybe we can just combine the two," Grayson said cryptically.

I raised an eyebrow. "What do you mean?"

"What's your scary story?" he prompted, eyes shining with playfulness.

I blushed and looked away, feeling silly. "You know, I actually don't have any. I grew up in Los Angeles, always in apartments and new-build houses. I guess I just never lived in a place old enough or spooky enough to invite a haunting into my life," I chuckled. "Sorry to disappoint. But what about you?"

"Oh, I've got one. But it's not supernatural or anything. Just pure Alaskan reality," he began, getting comfortable with one arm draped around my shoulders.

"I'm already on the edge of my seat," I replied, grinning.

"Okay, so let's set the stage," he said. "I was in high school, had a lot of buddies."

"I bet you were a hot jock, right?" I interjected.

He shrugged modestly. "I don't know about that. I've never been a big fan of labels. But I was athletic, yes. And so were most of my friends. We were all really into sports. Growing up in a place like Alaska, there's not a whole lot to do if you aren't at least a little bit sporty."

"Were you the school quarterback or something?" I asked.

Grayson laughed. "No. You have to remember, this is an Alaskan high school. Yeah, sure, we have football. But it's hockey that everybody gives a damn about."

"Ah, so you played hockey," I said, nodding.

"Yes. Along with my friends. We were all on the team together, and we were stiff competition for the other schools in the area. Rivalries get a little heated when there's nowhere else to blow off steam but in the hockey stadium," he explained. "So, this one time, my friends and I decided to pull a prank on an opposing school. We piled into my friend's ancient Jeep in the middle of the night and drove all the way out to our rival high school."

"Oh boy. I think I see where this is going," I said.

"Just wait," he said, eyes shining brightly. "So we knew it was too risky to park on campus. There were security cams, we assumed. Instead, we just parked on the far side of the woods that formed the side perimeter of the rival high school, and we walked through the woods. Our plan was to steal the mascot head. We were the polar bears, they were the grizzlies."

"I swear I've seen this movie before," I joked.

"But then, it got weird. We didn't even make it all the way through the woods before we ran into something. Something very large and very, very territorial," he said.

I gasped, eyes wide. "A bear?"

He nodded. "Yup. A big, bulky mama bear from the looks of her. Now, everybody who lives in Alaska ought to know better than to try and outrun a bear. They look like they would move slowly, but they're actually incredibly quick. They're all muscle. The best thing to do is make a lot of noise and try to scare the bear off while slowly backing away. But my buddies got spooked and started running," he said.

"Holy shit," I murmured. "What happened?"

"Well, I realized my friends were all taking off in one direction, and the bear was heading after them. But I knew the woods back there way better than my friends did. So I took initiative. I ran in the other direction, still pointing toward the way out, but in a roundabout way. And sure enough, that mama bear made the easy decision to try and chase down one solitary teen rather than a group of them," Grayson said.

"The grizzly chased you?" I burst out.

He smiled and nodded. "Yep. Full speed. I was darting in and out of the trees, doing everything I could to confuse her. Thing is, it was the middle of the night in the Alaskan woods. There was no source of light besides the moon, and it was hard to see where I was going. I knew one wrong move, one trip or tumble, could cost me my life. So I just kept running. I couldn't see where I was headed, but I moved on instinct. I could hear that mama bear behind me grunting and hustling through the woods, snapping tree branches and twigs in her path."

"My god," I breathed. "How did you get out?"

"I just didn't give up. I kept running, even though it felt like my heart was on fire. And finally, I made my way out of the tree line. I bolted down the highway toward where I knew the Jeep was parked. The bear was close on my heels when my buddies came rumbling up the road with the Jeep. They stopped just long enough for me to dive into the back seat. That bear took a swipe at me and managed to knock off one of my sneakers, it was that close," he related.

"Wow," I murmured, totally in awe. "That is definitely scarier than a ghost story."

"Just another day in the life of an Alaskan teenager," he chuckled.

"You're incredible, Grayson," I said honestly. "You blow my mind."

A mischievous grin spread across his face and he stood up, scooting to perch on the side of the Jacuzzi. He was slowly stroking his cock, getting it hard and erect for me as my mouth watered to taste it. With a curl of his finger beckoning me, he gave me my next command.

"I'll keep blowing your mind if you'll keep blowing mine," he growled.

That was all I needed to hear.

12

GRAYSON

AROUND NOON OF THE NEXT DAY, I WAS STANDING ON THE ROOF OF THE lodge—the roof proper, not just the towers. Landon was hovering around the edge of the roof and keeping an eye on the photoshoot in progress, but the roof's incline was so mild that we still had to clear off some of the snow before getting started.

The photographers wanted some shots of the guys with the mountains in the distance, and the best way to do that, they had decided, was to get everyone up on the roof and start taking pictures of them posing majestically and looking up at Denali. I had to admit, it was amusing. Chuck was taking shots of Ivan and Kristian, who were both shirtless and posing—one with a towel over his shoulders, the other kneeling down and looking out over the landscape as if he were an adventurer setting out on an expedition.

And naturally, all of their clothing was brand name, Chuck had a couple of bottles of a sports drink on hand to dramatically guzzle for the camera at the end of the shoot. I was starting to see why people thought this kind of job was fun.

But not every aspect of it was.

"I mean it, Milan, honestly," Connor was saying as I stood nearby, watching the scene unfold. "That was *not* your fault, don't blame yourself."

Milan was a towering gentle giant of a Serbian man with thick, curly hair and arms that could probably tear a phonebook in half. And at that moment, Connor and I had pulled him aside to console him while he had what Connor called "one of his mini-meltdowns."

"I didn't know the shirt was going to be that tight," his accented voice said, looking like he was on the verge of tears as Connor examined the rip in Milan's shirt at the back of the shoulders.

He had slipped into one of the sponsored brand outfits for the shoot, and one casual flex later, the fabric in the back had split like a ripe melon. When it first happened, Connor and I'd had to turn our faces to keep from laughing, but Milan apparently had a tendency to beat himself up for things like this. The poor guy was self-conscious about his size.

"It's fine," Connor said with a reassuring smile as Milan leaned against one of the stone chimney stacks. "We have a backup we can put on Niko later, and we'll get you a few shots with some of the workout equipment inside later."

"I like this brand," Milan said despondently, and Connor nodded, putting a hand on his shoulder.

"Did Chuck get a few shots of the damage?" I asked, tilting my head to the side and looking between the two.

"Of course, yeah," Connor said with a wave of his hand. "We photograph that kind of thing to send to accounting."

"You can still use that," I said with a gruff smile, and Milan raised an eyebrow at me before I explained. "Slip it back on, tear and everything, and look like you just flexed the shit out of it—send it to the advertiser. Sometimes we do that when our flying gear breaks, and the manufacturers like knowing the different ways their things can break."

"Like outsourcing," Connor said with a chuckle, nodding at Milan.

The musclebound Serbian nodded slowly, looking somewhat comforted by that as he looked to Connor. "You are thinking, is good, then?"

"You're doing them a favor," Connor said, nodding and shooting a grateful look to me. "Really, it's no inconvenience to anyone. Don't be so hard on yourself, the fact that we're even up here doing all this is better than I hoped we'd get out of the blizzard."

Milan seemed to be reassured by this, and he finally gave a half-smile and nodded to both of us.

"I'll find David, see if he hasn't thrown the shirt away yet," he decided. "Thank you, both."

He stomped off, leaving Connor and me to smile somewhat proudly to each other.

"Nice save," Connor said.

"Just told him the truth," I said with a chuckle.

"I just never would have thought a pilot's experience would be relevant to fitness modeling problems," he said with a grin, shaking his head as he watched the models start to shuffle themselves around for a new round of photos. "You're full of surprises."

"You didn't think someone crazy enough to want to be a bush pilot would be predictable, did you?" I asked with a grin, but before he could answer, I felt my phone buzzing at my hip.

I glanced down at it, surprised to hear it go off in the first place, and I saw my sister Heather's name on the screen. I looked up at Connor, who was already pointing over to the models.

"Got to take that? I'm going to go check on the shoot over there. Ivan and Kristian are exes, believe it or not, so I have to make sure things aren't getting to, ah, heated."

"Have fun with that," I said with a chuckle as Connor carefully walked across the roof over to the group while I made my way behind the chimney stack to take the call.

"Hey, Heather," I answered. "Everything alright?"

"Well, good to hear you're alive! I was just about to ask you the same thing," she said. "What's been going on up there? You never touched base when the snow stopped!"

I raised my eyebrows and opened my mouth to protest, but then it dawned on me that she was, in fact, right about that. I frowned at my own forgetfulness.

"Ah. Well, uh... you're not wrong," I admitted.

"Not wrong?" she blurted, not exactly incredulous but sounding more than a little surprised. "Uh, you sure you aren't going stir crazy up there? You're usually the one who checks in more regularly than anyone else."

"Well, that's normally because we have a job in progress around the corner and I'm not up to my neck in snow and models," I said, rubbing my chin as I glanced over my shoulder at the group.

Kristian and Ivan did appear to be in the middle of an argument that Connor was mediating while Chuck took a smoke break on the corner of the roof. I felt a smile tugging at my lips. I'd only been with them a few days, but part of me felt as comfortable around the group as I felt at work back home. Sure, they weren't exactly my people, but being in the same place together so much sometimes made me feel like Connor and I were shepherding around a big, weird family.

"Yeah, but I figured you'd be on the line nonstop with nothing else to do up there. Aren't you bored out of your mind?" she asked.

"Well, there's always a few things that need doing here and there," I said. "Landon and I had to batten down the hatches for these city boys," I said with a teasing grin over at the group, who was still out of earshot. "They wouldn't have known the first thing to do if I hadn't been here, so it's for the better that we got snowed in with them."

"Now that's not the Grayson I know," she said, sounding dangerously interested.

Fortunately, siblings had a way of knowing each other's weaknesses, such as how easy it was to get Heather distracted.

"No, I'll start sounding like Dad if I'm not careful," I admitted with a grin. "Speaking of, how's everyone back home?"

"Uh, Mom and Dad are good," she said, and I heard the sound of a chair leaning back while I slowly paced toward the opposite side of the roof. "They're still on that cruise down in Mexico. By the way," she added, "did you hear the news about Daniel?"

"What, are they moving the date again?" I asked.

"Ooooh, he didn't tell you! Shit," she said, but she was half-giggling nonetheless. "Okay, you have to act surprised when he talks to you, but he wants you to be the best man at the wedding."

My heart jumped, and I couldn't keep a smile off my face as I put my hand on my hip and stared down at the blanket of slowly melting snow smattered across the landscape below. I still remembered how much we'd celebrated when Daniel and Wes announced their engagement at the end of our little road trip. It was a damn good crown on an already great trip. It wasn't really a surprise that Daniel wanted me to be best man—it would have been either Caleb or me, after all. And neither of us would have felt stiffed if the other had been picked. In fact, we joked about both Caleb and me being best men at the same time.

"Well I'll be damned," I said.

"And if you can't keep a secret, throw the blame on someone else," she said in a joking tone. "I don't want to risk losing the Best Woman spot. Or is it grooms maid?"

"I don't think either family will be too picky," I said. "Then again, I think Wes could run the wedding however he wants and nobody would argue."

"You might be projecting a little," Heather teased, and I couldn't help but chuckle.

"Maybe a little," I admitted.

"Speaking of," Heather said, "Mom's starting to ask about *you* again. The other guys getting into relationships left and right has her saying 'innocently' she wants grandkids soon. Should we plan more fake dates for the wedding so she doesn't try to set us up with strangers again?"

My grin turned into something of a wince, and I ran a hand through my short hair. "So... about that," I said.

There was a pause on the other end of the line.

"You've got to be kidding me," Heather finally blurted flatly.

I was quiet around the guys at work, but Heather and I had always been open with each other—we were family, after all, and family in Kenai stuck close together.

"Now, before you say anything," I started, but Heather interrupted.

"You're serious!" she said. "It's that guy who came into the room with you and Landon, isn't it?"

I couldn't think of an excuse fast enough, not that I wanted to. I was grinning, knowing there wasn't much to do here but let Heather rant, because I wasn't about to try to hide Connor from her. I liked him too much to hide him.

"Okay, what in the actual hell is with you guys going out on jobs and coming back with boyfriends in the backseat?!" she said while I turned the speaker away from my mouth so I could laugh. "I hear you laughing! Is that all I have to do to get a husband? Fly somewhere and get stuck? Because I will get my pilot's license in, like, *no time*. You watch me."

"Hey, I won't stop you," I said, still grinning.

"And I'll make all three of you cover for me!" she added. "For *three* weeks!"

"To be fair, I think you have that much vacation time saved up," I said.

"Three weeks and two days, to be exact," she said smugly. "It's my secret weapon as payback for all the romance I've been missing out on. But hold on, *what*?! We need to back up," she said. "You and the model manager? The guy *from LA*?"

"You say that like it's..." I started but trailed off.

"The last thing anyone would have expected? Uh, yeah," she said. "C'mon details, let's go!"

After a few awkward moments trying to figure out how to start, I summarized the past few days' events for Heather in about as matter-of-fact a tone as I could. From the moment I had stepped into the first dinner to the photoshoots and up to today, I gave her the short, sweet, and censored version of what felt like me snatching Connor. And as I talked about it, my tone warmed up—I hadn't spent much time reflecting on how fast everything had happened.

When you were trapped somewhere like this, a few days felt like several weeks.

"Oh my god, you're like model-dads," Heather said, and I rolled my eyes.

"We are not model-dads," I clarified.

"I'm still adding 'model management' to your CV," she mumbled quickly and quietly. "In all seriousness, though, that sounds pretty amazing, dude. He sounds like a good guy."

"I wish I had him somewhere that wasn't as, uh, busy," I said, "Hard to get to know someone as much as you want when it's kind of like one long work day for him."

"Yeah, I was thinking that," she said, drumming her fingers on the desk. "Hmm. Well, if it were me, I'd see if I could get creative with the space economy. When I looked the lodge up, I saw it's kind of built to feel bigger inside than it is on the outside, so maybe there's somewhere you could set up to do something nice for him? You're surrounded by a bunch of hunky European guys, he'd probably like something that makes him feel special."

I raised my eyebrows. "You don't think he's jealous, do you?"

"I mean, I don't know the guy, and I'm not personally the jealous type," she said, "but if I was talking to a guy and surrounded by a bunch of runway models for a full week..."

"Sure," I admitted, "but Connor's... well, he's no lightweight himself."

"Yeah, but models are different," she said, somewhat reluctantly. "It's almost a status thing. I had a few model friends in college. It gets competitive in ways you wouldn't expect. Honestly, I wasn't even anywhere near that world, but just having friends who were made me a little self-conscious now and then."

"Well, when you put it that way..." I murmured, and I turned around to check on the group.

On the bright side, Kristian and Ivan didn't seem to be fighting anymore. In fact, they were having a cheerful conversation with Chuck, and the shoot appeared to be almost over. But Connor was nowhere to be seen.

"Hey, can I touch base later, Heather?" I asked. "I think we're moving around a little up here."

"Sure!" she said. "Yeah, damn, sounds like you've got your hands full up there. What's your timeframe looking like? We're going to need you in the air at the end of the week," she reminded me, and I winced.

"I'm keeping that in mind, but I'll be honest, that's the last thing I want to think about right now," I said, making my way toward the roof access door we used to get up here and waving to the group.

"Understood, boss," she said, snorting a laugh. "I'll uh, check in later. Stay warm."

"You too," I said, and we ended the call as I hurried downstairs to see where Connor had slipped off to.

The other models were milling around between the bars and the cafe now that the shoot was over and most of the day was done with, but I didn't see Connor at any of the loose groups that had formed. Asking around didn't turn up any results. The models I ran into hadn't seen him, and the journalist—who was making a rare trek out of his suite to the kitchen, just shrugged his shoulders as he slipped by me.

It was strange that he kept to himself so much. Even though he supposedly had some work to do while he was waiting for the shoot to be finished, I figured he'd at least spend some downtime with the others.

Then again, he could have just been a snob.

By the time I checked the third lounge, I shook my head and headed for the stairs, wondering if he had gotten a headache and gone to bed or something. But when I passed the doors to the gym, I came to a stop and looked through the glass at the sight of a lone figure by the rock-climbing wall.

It was Connor.

Furrowing my eyebrows, I pushed the door open and approached him. He had changed into gym clothes, and he looked up in surprise at the sight of me coming toward him and he blushed. He was wearing the harness for the rock-climbing wall... sort of. It wasn't buckled properly, and the right side was just kind of hanging loosely.

"Uh... hey!" he said, grinning sheepishly. "Did the shoot wrap up okay? It looked like everything was under control by the time I headed off."

"Everything was fine, yeah," I grunted, shrugging. "But what are *you* doing?"

"What do you mean?" he said, raising an eyebrow and giving an unconvincing smile. "I'd just remembered that since we've been getting so much work done off the cuff, I haven't really been working out as much as I usually do. Thought I'd squeeze in a little time on the wall before dinner."

I nodded slowly. It made sense, but something still seemed a little odd about the way he was fidgeting.

"So, the wall?" I asked, crossing my arms.

"I figured it would be just a low-intensity, all-over work out just to loosen up," he suggested, shrugging.

"Well, you're not wrong," I admitted. "Your technique could use some improvement, though," I added, reaching for his harness and starting to help get it straightened out.

"I might have been a little overeager," he said, wincing.

"And a little shady," I pointed out.

Connor opened his mouth to protest, but he blushed and averted his eyes. It was almost amusing to see a guy like him squirm the way he only could under me. But I didn't have to think too hard about what might have been making him anxious. I thought back to what Heather said about being surrounded by models whose career it was to look a very specific kind of beautiful and fit.

Connor was trying to pick up the slack. I gave a gruff smile. It was kind of adorable.

"Well, we've got some time before dinner," I said, walking over to one of the harnesses for myself. "Come on, I'll show you how to get up one of these things without busting your ass. It was one of the first things my friends and I did when we moved to Anchorage and hit the college gym."

Connor's face split into a grin, and he tilted his head to the side. "Really? That was the first thing you went for, too?"

I shrugged as I approached him. "Good workout. Fun. Rock

climbing kicks ass. Come on, let's get up there," I said, pinching him on the ass.

He shook his head, laughing and following after me as we got ourselves hooked up to spend the next half hour climbing over each other.

13

CONNOR

I WAS FEELING VERY APPREHENSIVE THIS AFTERNOON AS I SAT ON THE edge of the bed, pulling on a pair of thick, woolly socks and my boots. There was a lot to cover today, work-wise, and I was feeling sluggish. I kept catching myself gazing forlornly at the bedsheets, the cushy pillows that still faintly carried the distinctive masculine scent of the man who had been sleeping next to me. All I wanted was to kick these shoes back off, wriggle down under the sheets, and just daydream until I got sleepy enough to actually fall asleep. Oh, how tempting that sounded. I glanced at the clock on the nightstand and winced. I was used to hectic scheduling anyway: late nights, early mornings. Time was relative when creativity was involved. Sometimes a shoot would be over within a couple hours. But other times it would drag on all day and into the night. That was always frustrating, but also weirdly satisfying. It felt good to pour my whole self into my work, cheerleading and managing from the sidelines.

Not a great time to be off my A-game. I was supposed to prepare myself for a group meeting with Chuck and David to discuss alternative photo shoot ideas since our originally-planned, highly-organized, expensive outdoor shoot idea was clearly not going to happen anytime soon. At least today the sun was shining brightly in a lovely blue sky as the walls of snow began their steady decline. I groaned and flopped backward on the bed, staring up at the ceiling. I was trying to ignore the twisting sensation in my gut, that familiar old lick of anxiety that preceded every professional meeting like the one I was about to walk into. I was good at my job and I knew how to hold my own in a debate, but the beforehand moments were always the hardest.

Just as I was lying on the bed, pondering if there was any possible way I could escape (nope, snowed in, damn it), there was a soft knock at the door. I sat up straight and brushed off the front of my clothes even though they were perfectly clean.

"Um, come in!" I called out.

The door creaked open slowly and a large, powerful body stepped through the threshold. As usual, I almost gasped at how fucking gorgeous he was. Grayson, standing before me in his rugged clothing and light gear, his eyes piercing and so wide awake. I got the sense he was one of those people you could never catch off-guard. He was perfectly aware and prepared at all times. I liked to think of myself as having my shit together, but Grayson put me to shame. It was so subtle but undeniable—confidence in every move he made, every sauntering step he took. People naturally turned to him for guidance and assurance. He was so exciting and yet so comforting at the same time.

"Oh hey," I said, lacing up my boots. "How's your morning?"

"Just got back from a little maintenance work. One of the guest bathrooms had a leaky faucet, but I took care of it. No more dripping," Grayson remarked.

I beamed proudly at him. "Well, that was very helpful of you."

He shrugged. "As long as I'm here I might as well make myself useful," he said simply.

"You don't have to do that," I reminded him.

"Got to keep busy. That's one thing you learn quickly about getting snowed in—idle hands make for nervous company," he said.

I chuckled. "Never heard that one before."

"Yeah," he said with a smile, "it's just something my mom used to say on snow days. She said having us in the house cooped up with her while she was trying to get work done stressed her out. Heather and I were pretty active kids, as you can probably imagine. So she was constantly helping us find ways to pass the time and enjoy our snow day."

"And stay out of her way, I presume," I quipped.

He laughed, a deep, sonorous sound that instantly put me at peace. "Yes, exactly."

Grayson came over to sit down next to me. "So, what's on the docket for this morning?"

I sighed. "Just a meeting with the photographers to discuss other ideas to replace the expensive outdoor shoot we had planned for. Not looking forward to this, to be perfectly honest."

Grayson frowned slightly. "Why? What's the problem?"

"It's just a lot of responsibility. There's so much riding on this excursion to Alaska, and that outdoor shoot was supposed to be the pinnacle of the whole project. A substantial amount of money has been poured into this, and now that we can't cash in on that for the outdoor shoot, we're going to have a hell of a time replacing it," I explained, already feeling more anxious as I talked about it more.

Truth be told, I had kind of been pushing it out of my mind. I was in denial, which was out of character for me. Then again, I had been a little distracted lately. There was no mystery as to why. He was sitting right in front of me. He was quiet for a moment, clearly deep in thought. Then he stood up and offered me a hand. I raised an eyebrow at him quizzically as I accepted his hand.

"What? You have a look in your eye," I remarked warily.

"I'm going with you," he declared.

"What?" I snorted. "No. That's not necessary. I'll figure it out."

"You need me in there," Grayson insisted. "I can help come up with ideas, give you all some insight from an outsider's point of view."

I smiled softly, tilting my head to one side. "Grayson, you're a pilot. Why would you even want to get involved in this kind of thing? Wouldn't it just bore you to tears?" I asked.

"Well, you'll be there, so I think I'll have enough to entertain me," he said smoothly.

I blushed, just as he knew I would. "Alright, fine. You wore me down. But don't get too offended when Chuck and David make a big deal out of it," I said, following him out of the bedroom and into the hallway. Grayson looked at me over his shoulder with a big, mischievous grin.

"I've come face to face with a mama bear, remember? Chuck and David don't scare me in the least," he asserted firmly. "I can handle it, Connor. Don't you worry."

"I trust you," I told him, and I was surprised to find that I meant it. But of course I did.

It was a bit of a walk across the sprawling lodge to the empty restaurant, where the meeting was to be held. During the walk, Grayson let his hand brush against mine a few times, and each time my heart fluttered wildly in my chest. That was all it took: one light, passing touch, and I was enraptured. There was just something about him that drew me like a moth to a flame, but less destructive. On the contrary, with every step I took side by side with the most amazing man I'd ever met, I felt my confidence building, my brain relaxing and settling into gear for the meeting. I could handle this. For sure. I had dealt with bad work outcomes before, and this time I had the added help of Grayson. I wasn't sure what he could bring to the table exactly, but as long as he knew, that was fine by me.

As we walked in, my stomach began to twist into knots. Chuck and David were already there in the empty restaurant area, sitting across from each other at a corner table near the bar. The door behind the bar that connected with the kitchen was wide open, and I could see that Landon was in there. I squinted, trying to figure out why, until I noticed the smell of food cooking. Butter and garlic sizzling.

"Is he…?" I murmured aside.

Grayson nodded. "Yeah, Landon's got a real knack in the kitchen."

"Right! I'm still amazed he can do that, but you don't hear me complaining," I replied.

"Oh hey! Over here!" called out Chuck from across the restaurant, waving at us.

As usual, Chuck looked fairly jovial, but David was pensive, staring at Grayson like he was trying to do math in his head or something. I could tell he was confused as to why the non-cooking pilot had tagged along, but I was not about to bring it up myself. I figured Grayson could do well enough by himself if he wanted to talk about it. Grayson sat next to Chuck and I slid in next to David, who looked mildly relieved to be sitting next to me. I had a feeling he was still a little wary of Grayson. David was a chronic over-thinker—a trait that made him a productive artist but a slightly paranoid friend from time to time. Landon came out and brought us each a cold beer to sip while he cooked us what smelled like some kind of lemony, garlicky pasta with grilled chicken.

"Alright, so," Chuck began, leaning forward and cracking his knuckles, "let's get thinking."

"Anybody have any ideas? Anything at all?" David asked. He sounded considerably more stressed out, but that was pretty on-brand for him.

"Well, what was the point of the main shoot?" Grayson spoke up.

There was a deep pause and I fought the urge to wince.

David squinted at him. "The point?"

Grayson sighed. "Yes. What was the motivation? What elements were you hoping to capture?"

"The outdoor kind," Chuck remarked, taking a sip of his beer.

"Ha-ha. Very helpful," I said good-naturedly. "I think our main interest in coming to Alaska was to capture the vastness and the majesty of the landscape, using it as a backdrop to make our athlete models appear even more heroic and powerful than usual."

Grayson snapped his fingers, grinning. "Yes! That's what I'm looking for. Dig deep."

David seemed to be warming up to this method of brainstorming. Chuck was amused, sitting back in his chair, watching us all wrack our brains.

"I was looking forward to doing some harsh-lighting shoots where the sun was reflecting off the snow, washing everything out. Most photographers consider that a bad thing, but I think if used right, it can be an intriguing effect," David mused aloud.

"I was hoping to get some swimwear shots," Chuck said. "You know, take it to the extreme, show that these guys are tough enough to withstand posing half-nude in the snow. The juxtaposition of hot and cold, comfortable versus intolerable. The fitness mags eat that shit right up."

"Let's not give our models hypothermia, please," David quipped.

"He has a point there," Grayson agreed firmly. "Don't risk frostbite for a shot."

"I'm sure we can figure out a way to accommodate some version of all these things indoors," I asserted, the ideas starting to flow to me. "What is important to me is that these shoots provide variety and range for my models' portfolios. I need them to look polished. I need them to look innovative, but still mainstream. Marketability is everything these days, and my clients have strictly curated social media feeds, news access—all that behind the scenes stuff."

"And if they succeed, we succeed," David added.

"I'll drink to that," Chuck laughed, raising his beer glass.

We all clinked and continued chatting about our plans, fleshing out some ideas and bouncing them back and forth. Eventually, Landon came out of the kitchen with five plates of food. He sat down at the end of the table and listened as we discussed what to do.

"I really would like to take the time and do some individual shoots," David said.

"Yeah, that would be nice. Just take it slow and be methodical about it," Chuck agreed.

"What if we give each model a little interview?" I suggested. "Just gather together a short bio for each guy. Talk about their work, their self-discipline, the keys to their fitness and success, what drives and inspires them every day."

"That's a fantastic idea," Chuck remarked.

"Yes, it is," Grayson said, and the look in his eyes made my heart skip a beat. He was proud.

"And we can personalize the shoot to fit each model," David went on. "It'll help fill out the magazine spread, plus it'll propel the models' brands."

"Exactly," I said cheerily.

"Everybody wins," Chuck said.

The conversation meandered on for an hour or so longer, all of us happily discussing ideas while chowing down on the absolutely divine pasta dish Landon had whipped up for us. I was impressed by the man's abilities in the kitchen. There was no doubt about his skill. Throughout the discussion, Grayson supported me at every turn, lifting up my ideas, affirming my directions. It felt good. Really good. He believed in me, and that was an honor I didn't know I even deserved. Toward the end of the discussion, Grayson nudged my shoulder subtly and caught my eye. Without having to say a word, I knew he wanted for me to go with him when he left. We scooted out, said our goodbyes, and then he led me out of the restaurant.

"Where are we going?" I asked as soon as we were out of earshot of the guys.

"If I say the basement, will that freak you out?" he teased.

My eyes widened, but I scoffed. "As long as you're not planning to murder me down there."

"Oh, I wouldn't dream of it. But the ghost that lives down there might," he hissed.

"Ha-ha. Yeah. I'd love a ghoul to try and take me on right now. After that meeting, I feel good. Really good, Grayson. I could fight a ghost right now, no problem," I said.

"Well, good. I'll leave that to you then," he chuckled.

We followed down a long, winding hallway to the rather ominous door that led down to the basement. It was dimly lit and smelled musty, but that was to be expected. It was a basement, after all. I coughed as we took the stairs down into the darkness. I wrinkled my nose, grateful that Grayson was walking in front of me. He walked across the basement to a ladder built against the wall, a little trapdoor above it in the ceiling.

"You've got to be kidding me," I said, shaking my head.

He laughed. "I know. It looks bad. But trust me, it's worth it."

"You're lucky I do trust you. I would not do this for just anyone," I replied. "That said... you go first, Grayson."

"Gladly," he said.

He hoisted himself up onto the ladder and climbed up the few rungs effortlessly, pushing up the trapdoor and climbing up inside. I could smell the faint, but distinct scent of chlorine and I was instantly intrigued. I heard him stand up, brush off his hands, and sigh contentedly. I walked over to look up through the ceiling, rolling back and forth on my heels. Grayson turned and crouched down, peering down at me with an amused expression.

"Come on up. Do you need help?" he said.

I puffed my chest out in defiance. "No! No. I got it. Just... give me a second," I murmured.

I grabbed hold of the ladder and climbed up, looking around as I stood up next to Grayson.

"What the hell is this?" I asked.

"Secret hot tub room," he remarked, grinning. "I found it the other day when I was rummaging through the basement. Figured if we want a little alone time, where better than this?"

"So nobody really knows this is here?" I asked, dumbfounded.

He shrugged. "If they do, nobody has mentioned it to me."

"Our chances of getting caught are pretty low then, right?" I said. I turned around to see that Grayson was walking toward a far corner of the little room. Curious, I followed him.

Then I stopped in my tracks, surprised by what I was seeing. There in the corner was perhaps the coziest little nook I had ever seen. Pillows and blankets piled high, the reflection of the hot tub water playing peacefully across the ceiling. It was like a cuddle puddle with a light show attached.

"Wow, this is... this is really sweet," I said, rendered almost speechless.

He reached under a pillow and pulled out a glass bottle. Red wine.

"You think of everything," I said. I couldn't stop grinning.

"Yes, I did," he said, curling his finger and beckoning for me to come with him.

My whole body felt like electricity as I crossed the room and melted into the pillow pile in Grayson's arms, and I had to wonder if this was as close to heaven as I'd ever get. I reached for the wine, but he pulled it away just to keep it out of reach with a meaningful smile on his face.

"If you want it," he growled. "You'll need to work for it."

I narrowed my eyes defiantly at him, but before I could reply, he set the bottle down and pounced on me. Rolling in the pillows, my laughter turned to a soft moan as he groped my cock and kissed my mouth, the waters of the hot tub dancing along the dim interior of our little hideaway.

Soon, he had managed to put a thick thigh on either side of me, pinning me down as he slid his belt off. He took each of my wrists and used the belt to tie them behind my head, restraining me and exposing my mouth to him entirely when he opened his pants and withdrew his thick cock.

It hit the side of my cheek, and I let my mouth fall open as he guided it into my lips, letting me look up at his gorgeous, muscular body towering over me. Just feeling imprisoned by him warmed my skin, making me feel like he could keep me here forever if he wanted to. It would have just been me, Grayson, and every last one of his primal cravings.

That was the only thing missing from this little slice of paradise.

He took my head in his hands, and I felt the weight of his cock as it slid past my lips and onto my tongue. I didn't dare close my eyes. I wanted to look up at my conqueror, see every change in his face as the tip of my tongue danced along his thick trunk. He glared down at me, equal parts lustful and carefully making sure I didn't step out of line. I knew the pace he liked, and I groaned into it as I felt his cock pulse in my mouth.

He started to slide back and forth very carefully, and it was my job to make sure every second of it was pure bliss for my controlling captor. I tasted precome, and I felt a rewarding rush at the knowledge that I was pleasing him the way he deserved.

I started picking up my pace, and Grayson's mountain of a body reacted. His cock was starting to tighten, and I felt his nails scrape across my scalp before the first burst of him entered my mouth. I strained at my "bindings" and squirmed my body under him, letting him feel every bit of me as I sucked him.

When it was over, I tasted one last drop of it before he slid out of me, and he slowly slid his belt off my wrists while his husky panting filled the room.

"Better than wine," I remarked, smiling up at him as he brought my wrist to his mouth and kissed it.

"Hopefully not so good that you're not thirsty anymore," he said with a chuckle as he planted a kiss on my cheek. "Because I'm not planning on leaving this place without emptying this bottle."

"I can drink to that," I said as he helped me up to enjoy the date.

14

GRAYSON

The camera snapped, and Ivan let his dignified yet imposing posture relax into a more easygoing one, leaning against the mantle with one hand while looking into the fire with a thoughtful expression. The camera snapped again.

"Beautiful," Chuck said in a soft murmur.

"Chuck is pretty reluctant to give compliments," Connor whispered to me across the room at the kitchen counter where we were standing, and Connor was making a few snacks for the team. "That's impressive."

He was standing beside me, in the process of making ten large, piping-hot mugs of cocoa with just enough rum splashed into them to give them the kick we all needed. I stood by wearing my gym clothes, since I planned on working out a little after making sure Connor had a handle on everything.

The rest of the models had been completely on board with the idea we'd come up with. In fact, they had been eager enough to get started that we had already made a decent amount of headway by the time we started making cocoa.

"The idea behind these shots," Connor explained to me, "is that some of these shots will get used later alongside these sort of miniature-interviews that Pete Russo is doing upstairs."

"Surprised the journalist hadn't frozen or something, we see him so little," I said.

"Oh god, don't joke like that," Connor said with a mild laugh. "But yes. These are big for the models, too. These are going to be incredible for their portfolios, especially since we're not getting absolutely everything we could have out of this week."

I raised an eyebrow at Connor. He was his usual self, highly composed and speaking in clear, round tones that could carry across the whole room if he wanted them too. But every now and then, he'd slip something that made me wonder if I needed to be paying closer attention to my man. I nodded, but I picked up my own mug of cocoa and took a drink and didn't call him out just yet.

Connor raised an eyebrow at me and smirked. "Is there any cocoa left in that?"

"No," I admitted, swirling it around. "Mostly rum. Only way I have any chance of feeling a little loosened up."

"Really? Had you figured for a complete lightweight," Connor said with playful sarcasm, looking my towering figure up and down.

"Didn't say it was a good thing," I added. "My bar tabs are no joke."

"Hey, it's not like we have to drink through a few awkward first dates anymore," he said with a wink, and I grinned after him as he made his way back over to the models.

He started talking to small groups of them, I assumed to touch base or organize something to do with the shoot. While he glided from model to model and coached each one for a bit, I got to sit back and admire the sight of him doing what he loved doing.

Connor might have looked like a deer in the headlights when I stomped in to tell him a blizzard was on his hands, but he knew how to talk people through these kinds of things, and that was a valuable skill indeed.

But there was still that slight tension in the way he moved that only I seemed to notice. He moved just quickly enough and with just enough care in his every step that I could tell he was more anxious than he was letting on. It made sense. There was a lot of pressure to perform on the one thing that was technically going according to schedule, even if we just made that schedule up this morning. And the photographers were agreeable but having the looming threat of the journalist hanging over Connor's head probably made up for that.

"Are you doing one too?"

David's voice caught me by surprise, and I looked over to see the younger photographer near the window, looking curiously over at me.

"Huh?" I asked, coming closer to the group.

"An individual shoot," David said, looking confused.

"Oh—no, David, he's not—" Connor started, turning away from Diego to hurry toward us, but he stopped halfway and pursed his lips, looking at me thoughtfully. "I mean... now that you mention it, I'm sure we *could*. If you want to," Connor added to me, trying desperately not to blush any more than he already was.

Normally, that would have been a solid, flat-out no from me, but the look on Connor's face gave me pause. He was into the idea in the kind of way that left him hot and bothered, and the idea of stoking that fire just a little was enticing.

"Yeah," I said, grinning at David. "Just for fun, right?"

"Whatever you want to use them for," David said, giving a lopsided grin after looking between me and Connor. "Okay, it's fine if you've never modeled before, this will be easy. What I want you to do is—"

Without being asked, I stripped my shirt off and tossed it over my shoulder, striding toward the kitchen. I pulled one of the benches out and propped a leg up on it, folding my arms over the knee and glaring at the camera like a lumberjack who'd just been interrupted from a hard day's work.

"Like this?" I grunted.

Connor's face went red, and he turned to take a drink of Diego's rum and cocoa while David lined up a shot and started rapid-fire snapping.

"Oh, yeah, sure!" he said. "That's great!"

"Another by the windows," I said, gesturing to the full-wall window that was still largely covered in snow on the outside.

David followed me while I posed against it, feeling the cool ice outside chill my skin, but I stood out in warm contrast to the rest of the white, cold backdrop.

"Wow," he said, genuinely surprised. "Connor, our pilot is kind of a natural. Yeah, Grayson, now give me—okay, that works, hell yeah!"

I had turned to put my arms against the wall as if resting against it after a hard workout, and even some of the other models were looking over, and out of the corner of my eye, I could see Connor looking at me like he was having a religious experience. The more I posed for the camera, the more I got into it, shamelessly showing off the muscles I'd built up over a lifetime of hard work and rugged living. I didn't do it because I liked showing off my body. To Connor, that was true, but I was no showoff.

No, I was doing this because Connor adored it. And the other models seemed to be enjoying a less serious shoot, too.

"Fuck yeah, tear it up!" Andrew called to me as I stretched out against the fireplace and got a few shots of me looking over my shoulder with the cinders in the background.

"I'm *living* for this," Niko said.

Connor couldn't tear his eyes away the entire time. He tried to keep an eye on Chuck's shoots a few times, but he found himself distracted, but in a way that he clearly needed. He had a smile on his face, his body language was more relaxed, and he wasn't even the only one enjoying seeing this side of me.

It wasn't a side I showed often, but I didn't mind reminding the photographers who was boss if it meant taking some pressure off Connor.

"Okay, I think that's going to do it," David said when he lowered the camera for the last time, still watching me with stars in his eyes and a glance to Connor. "Just a couple more to do with the others, but we're just about done here. Sure he's not a model? He ought to be."

"After this week, I think anything might be possible, but I wouldn't hold your breath for that one," Connor said with a soft laugh as I rolled my shoulders back and cracked my knuckles. "What do you think, Grayson?"

"I think I wouldn't mind a photographer coming by the hangar sometime if you want more of this," I said, gesturing to myself in general, "but I think if you want me for that kind of thing long-term, you might need to look somewhere else, I'm not letting myself get grounded anytime soon."

"Might take you up on that first part," David said, chuckling. "We'll edit these later. I definitely want you to be there for that."

"Sure thing, if I have time," I said, giving him a noncommittal nod and watching him turn to go flag down some of the other models before I turned to Connor. "Now, as for you..."

Connor's eyebrows went up, and even though he was still in his professional, managerial mode, just one good look from me was enough to make the seams start to crack in the best ways for both of us. I started to approach him slowly. He glanced over my shoulder at the others, but I had already checked on them before rounding on Connor: they were all distracted by the photographers talking to them in the other room. That meant Connor was all mine.

I reached around his waist and grabbed his ass, and I used the other hand to seize his tie. I was still shirtless, wearing nothing but my shoes and a pair of shorts that were not going to do a proper job of hiding the swelling between my legs. That was a problem I would need to deal with soon, unless I wanted to make things awkward with the group.

"What about me?" Connor asked, his tone still professional, but he was starting to sense what my intentions were, and I wasn't making it easy for him to slip away from me.

I advanced on him until we started to move into the shadows, and I watched the last light from the fireplace fading from his beautiful, wary face as I moved toward him.

"You put me on the spot back there," I growled. "You ran a good show, but that was awfully defiant of you, don't you think?"

He licked his lips and cast another furtive look toward the group, but I had Connor to myself for the time being, and I was planning to take full advantage of it—and him.

"You certainly didn't seem to mind," he said, giving me those wide, shining eyes that made it hard for me to be gruff with him, but I knew how good he could be at pushing me in just the right ways. "In fact, if I were a gambling man, I'd bet you even had some honest to goodness fun back there," he added with a defiant smirk.

I'd have to nip that in the bud, I decided.

Both of my hands reached forward and hooked their fingers under Connor's belt, and I slowly dragged him toward me to close the distance. I glared down at him for a few moments, narrowing my eyes and looking at him as if wondering just what to do with him this time.

"If you think that makes a difference," I said in a rumbling tone, "you haven't been paying attention."

I took him by the tie and tugged him along, and we made a careful escape from the area where the group was milling around to head back up to the suites. But instead of heading for Connor's this time, I took him toward mine.

"I need to hit the shower," I said, "and you're coming with me."

Before he could answer, I pulled him into the room with me and shut the door to pin him against the other side of it. I had barely been able to keep my hands off him. Our lips crashed together as I slid my hand up into his blond hair and stroked it, groaning as his lips melted against mine.

My cock had already swollen, and through the thin, breathable fabric of my shorts, there was even less to keep him from feeling everything that I wanted him to. I pushed my hips forward so my stiff cock could grind across his waist, and I gripped his shirt, letting out a low rumble as I felt the button-down that had overstayed its welcome.

The kiss broke, and I watched Connor's panting face look up at me with more than just lust. He was watching me carefully, regarding every detail in my face, reading me.

"You have something on your mind," I pointed out. "Tell me."

"I just..." he said, watching me thoughtfully. "I can't get over how much confidence you seem to put off. It just kind of radiates off you. I can't be the first person to have told you that."

"So do you," I pointed out, squeezing his ass.

"That's not the same," he said, smirking.

"Maybe not exactly," I admitted with a gruff, loving smile. "You're not getting anywhere far out of hand as long as I'm holding the reins up here. But those men out there listen to you just like they listen to me. Maybe not with as much fear," I half-joked, "but they listen. Because you know what you're doing with them. Just like I know what I'm doing with you," I added in a low tone.

"You're a hard act to follow, I'll give you that," he said.

"Good thing I'm the only man you need to be following right now," I said, and I slipped his tie off him and threw it over my shoulder.

His buttons came next, one after the other, and I stripped Connor as if he were a prize to unwrap. He was like my payment for this job, and I was going to make him worth the effort. I slid his shirt off his shoulders, then let his pants drop to his ankles to step out of them, and the rest of our clothes were left behind us in a scattered trail to the en suite shower.

I turned the hot water on and stepped inside, feeling it wash away the day in a wave of relaxing warmth that ran over my body generously. Hot water never seemed to run out here, and the pressure was perfect. Each en suite was almost as good as a sauna in its own right.

Once I was inside, I turned to Connor's naked form and beckoned him closer.

As soon as he was in reach, I pulled him against me and closed the shower doors. I cupped his face in my hands and kissed him, feeling that slick jawline in the hot water that doused us while I drew him closer. I groaned into him, happy to feel our cocks stiff and warm against each other again.

"This is where you belong," I growled. "At my side. In my arms. In my grasp," I emphasized, "where I can do whatever I want with you."

"I'm finding it harder and harder to argue with that," Connor admitted, and I reached down to take both of our cocks in a hand and squeeze them firmly.

"That won't stop you from trying, if I know you," I growled, and he shivered as my thumb brushed over the tips of our cocks together.

"Really, though," he said with a less playful but more sincere voice. "Thank you, for earlier."

"That was nothing," I dismissed in a single chuckle.

"It wasn't nothing," he said, smiling. "I know that kind of thing isn't your 'world' or whatever you want to call it. You went out on a limb to get involved with mine. I appreciate that."

My smile softened, and I brought his chin up to look him in the eye.

"I appreciate that limb being there," I said, then squeezed him to remind him I was still holding us. "But you know I'm not about to let go of it until I'm good and done."

I stroked our cocks together for emphasis, and this time, I reached into his hair and pulled it back to expose his neck and start to grind against him. It was sloppy, steamy fooling around, and each time our wet shafts pulsed against each other and Connor let out a soft gasp of pleasure, I felt my heart pounding in desire.

"I could do this to you all day," I said in a low, husky voice when I tore my lips from his neck. "But I dragged you in here so you could sit on my cock, and that's what you're going to do."

I pulled him toward the large tiled block of a seat in the large shower and sat myself down before reaching for the packaged condom and lube I'd set aside. After putting them on, I turned Connor's body around, sizing him up like a piece of meat and licking my lips before sliding a finger to his ass. I felt around his rim before sliding it in down to the knuckle, and Connor grabbed the railing on the wall as he gasped, almost clenching around me.

"Tense," I pointed out, teasing him as a second finger joined the first.

"You keep me on my toes," he admitted.

I chuckled and took him by the hips to slowly lower him onto my bulging crown. My cock found his hole easily, and he let out a low moan as I slowly worked my way into him. Inch by inch, I slid into his body and brought him closer to me until I could feel his firm, round cheeks against my hips. I reached around to his cock and started pumping it relentlessly as we rocked back and forth, and Connor's body was so tense that I felt him shudder involuntarily now and then.

He was a mess, but he was *my* mess.

"Fuck," he groaned. "Grayson... you're going so—"

I rutted into him harder, sliding back and forth with mechanical precision. My muscles worked together to deliver everything Connor had been lusting after downstairs, and I wasn't going to leave him to ache a minute longer. I was going to show him how easily I could take his stress away from him.

Connor gasped as I succeeded, and moments later, I felt the white-hot surge of pressure flow through me as I let my head lean back and give a husky groan. My come pulsed into him shot after shot, and Connor's release came hard and forcefully. The orgasm wracked my every nerve, and even before it was over, I held Connor tight to me, letting it all spill out.

And all I could think was that this week was coming to an end far too soon.

15

CONNOR

BY THE TIME THE DAY WAS STARTING TO WIND DOWN, IT WAS CLEAR THAT everyone was dog tired, but in the best way possible. There was a heavy aura of contentment and self-satisfaction. Everybody had gotten their moment to shine. Everyone had gotten to work out their tension and stress from being cooped up in the lodge for days. It was amazing how relaxed we all felt now that the biggest and most important shoot was over. I could sense that everyone felt confident about the results, but we still all wanted to gather around the various laptops in the communal living room to look at the photos from the day, and from the week in general.

One by one, everyone went to their respective rooms and came back having retrieved pillows and blankets, all changing into much comfier clothing. There were pajama pants, t-shirts, woolly thick socks, even a few pairs of house slippers. Chuck was wearing a massively oversized UCLA sweatshirt and David had a blanket wrapped around his shoulders like some kind of medieval peasant on a journey. We all piled up on the various sofas and chairs, some of us on pillows scattered on the floor, all curved around the coffee table where Chuck and David had their laptops open. On the other side of them was the fireplace, where a crackling, comforting fire was brightly lit and casting a sleepy orange glow over everything. From my spot on the end of the loveseat, I could look out the window. Outside, there was a heavy flurry of snowflakes falling almost horizontally in the icy wind. It was beautiful in a forbidding kind of way.

It certainly made the interior coziness around me feel even more sumptuous and relaxing by contrast. I was certainly grateful to be indoors, enjoying the warmth of the fire and the camaraderie of my team, who had definitely become more like friends over the course of our time here. As it turned out, getting locked into a lodge with a group of people with no way out and nothing much to do was a quick way to learn how to get along. And we did. Splendidly. I was surprised at the lack of drama, the ease with which we all fell into step and worked together like a team rather than a motley crew of competitive egos. I leaned back, yawning as I stretched my arms up over my head. I was going to sleep well tonight, that was for sure.

"I can't wait to see these photos," Diego said brightly from his perch on one end of the sofa. He rubbed his hands together, grinning.

"I know. I have a good feeling about this set," Niko remarked.

"You guys really pulled it together," Milan added, looking at David and Chuck.

"Couldn't have done it without you all, of course," Chuck replied. "And Connor. You guys should have seen him at our meeting. He was on fire."

"We all were. I think we just work well together," David agreed.

"Some of the poses you were pulling out looked straight-up editorial," Erik gushed. "Sal, remember when you balanced on those exercise balls. I still don't know how you did that."

"Looked like magic to me," Tomas laughed.

"Thick thighs, all muscle," another model said, gesturing at his legs.

"You got that right," Erik murmured, his eyes wide and his cheeks blushing. Poor guy. I knew he had a bit of a weakness for the bodybuilder types. He was a goner.

"Look at this one," Chuck said, pointing to the laptop screen.

"Ooh, damn," Niko said with a low whistle. "You really worked it, Sal!"

"Looks good to me. I don't know much about the technical side," Salvatore said in his beguiling Italian accent.

Erik stared at him like he was lit with the sun from within. I wondered warmly if that was how I looked when I was looking at Grayson. Speaking of which, I couldn't help but sing his praises to the others, even when he wasn't in the room to hear it.

"Grayson came up with a lot of helpful ideas, too," I piped up.

"Oh yeah, he impressed me with his ability to adapt and figure things out," David said.

That was high praise coming from David, who was usually a little tricky to please. He was a good-natured guy, but quiet. It took a lot for him to speak up for someone like that. It made my heart feel all fuzzy and sweet, knowing that my colleagues all seemed to not only approve of Grayson but actually like him. That told me he really was as great a guy as I saw him to be through my admittedly rose-tinted glasses. But he was the real deal. Grayson deserved the hype.

"Where is Grayson right now?" Paolo asked.

"And Landon?" added Andrew.

"They're out clearing the snow down to the main road," I informed them.

"Yikes. They've been gone for hours," Niko said, sounding genuinely worried for them.

I nodded. "I know. But you have to remember that they're from around here. They have a little bit more tolerance to the cold than you all do," I reminded him.

"It gets pretty cold in Germany," Erik said, shrugging.

"Not Alaska-cold," Chuck laughed. "Hey guys, check out this shot of Milan."

It was a sharp image of Milan back-bending over a hurdle, the bright lights reflecting off his rippling muscle, his finely-outlined abdominals. Admittedly, his package was pretty clearly on display, too, but we were all professional enough not to focus on that. Out loud. What we could do, though, was compliment every other aspect of the photo, which we were all too eager to do. We were in good moods, feeling comfortable and warm in the living room, like one giant sleep-over party. The compliments flowed as easily as the beer, and before long, we were all shouting our compliments and hyping each other up, getting buzzed with rosy cheeks and permanent, cheek-aching grins.

"Whoa!"

"So crisp!"

"The perspective in this shot is wild!"

"What a striking composition!"

It was just a round-robin of support and encouragement, the mood in the room getting higher and lighter with every shot we looked at. I couldn't help but smile as I looked around the room, feeling like I might just float away with happiness. It reminded me of being back in university dorms, gathering with all my fellow art and photography-loving friends in the communal hang-out space. We would put up a projection screen and flip through rolls and rolls of cheap film bought at yard sales and online auctions. We would build each other up, offering constructive criticism, always served up with wholesome, good intentions and often with a pinch of encouragement to balance it out. I had never before had such a productive and creative group of friends before, and it really taught me that one of the parts I loved most about being involved with the artistic community was the ability to form bonds and connect on a personal level with other creators.

I liked being the diplomat. The go-between. I liked navigating social situations and learning the quirks and tendencies of new friends, new colleagues, new clients. I even genuinely enjoyed answering emails all day long. The connection with other people was important to me. It was why I loved the opportunity my job gave me to really get to know a client and help book them for jobs that would not only advance their career but also assert and stimulate their own creative voice. It was rewarding for me to take an idea, a dream, and help support it until it could blossom into a reality. I helped people make their dreams come true, even in my small way, and that felt pretty damn good for me. I only wished that Grayson was here with me in this golden moment. Things were just plain better when he was experiencing them with me.

Then, almost as though my desires had summoned him, we all heard the telltale thud of heavy boots by the front door. The door unlocked and swung open, letting in a gust of cold air and howling wind, wrapped around the two heavily-bundled up but still hot as hell pilots. Landon came walking in first, whipping off his knitted hat and tossing it jock-like to Erik on the couch, making several of the models laugh. Landon was rosy-cheeked and smiling, and I could understand why the other guys were ogling him so much. But when Grayson stepped through the door behind him, I nearly fell off the loveseat.

He had the ruddy, wind-whipped face of a man who had just stared freezing cold temperatures in the eyes and fought them down. His hair was ruffled, with flecks of sparkling white snow dotting the locks. Grayson looked like some kind of bizarrely sexy yeti, coated in snow and quickly shedding layers of clothing as he turned and shut the door behind himself. He looked around at the room full of cuddled-up, cozy people and smiled with amusement.

"Looks like a middle school sleepover in here," he teased.

"Oh, like you don't want to join in," Chuck joked.

Landon sauntered over to sit on the floor, resting his back against Erik's legs. He glanced up at Grayson and shrugged, gesturing for him to join the pack.

"It's pretty warm and cozy by the fire. I might actually start to get the feeling back in my hands if I stay close by," Landon said, getting comfortable.

Andrew slipped off the loveseat and sat on the floor, making room for Grayson beside me. I winked up at him and saw a fleeting flicker of a smile on his face before he grunted in the affirmative and took the seat next to me. I scooted closer to him and rested against him, trying to pass some of my body heat to him. It was hard to resist the urge to brush the snowflakes out of his hair, but I figured that might be slightly too intimate for a group setting.

"So, what's it like out there?" Milan asked, wide-eyed and curious.

"Cold as fuck," Landon remarked. "But we made it happen."

"The path to the road from the lodge is now cleared," said Grayson.

Various cheers and whistles went around the room.

"That's good news!" David said happily.

"Great news," Chuck agreed.

"You guys are incredible for doing that," I said.

"It's not a fun job, but hey, somebody's got to do it," Landon remarked. "Might as well be the guys whose jobs don't depend on them looking pretty."

"I'd like to think I'm more handsome than pretty," Salvatore goaded.

"You're both, Sal, don't worry," Diego said, patting him on the shoulder.

"And it looks like some of the locals are clearing the snow from their properties, too. Before long, we should be back in business," Grayson announced.

"As usual, Alaskans rise up and do what's necessary," I said in awe.

Grayson looked at me with such intense and unexpected admiration when I said those words that for a moment, I felt like time stopped. All else ceased to exist. The world dropped away and left only that one golden, shining beacon through the darkness. He had always been a hero, from the first day we met until now. I kept waiting for the other shoe to drop, for his dark Prince Charming perfection to slip and reveal something less amazing underneath. Surely a man like Grayson was too good to be true. I just couldn't imagine a universe in which he and I got to exist at the same time. I felt an overwhelming rush of emotion as he looked at me. It was only a split second, but somehow I saw so far beyond that second. A future, stretching out across the vast horizon, intertwining Grayson's world and mine in a harmonious blend.

* * *

THE NEXT MORNING, Grayson had already gotten dressed and headed downstairs by the time I was ready and coming down to the front lounge to find him. I saw him peering out the curtain with a furrowed brow, and I descended the stairs with a sleepy wave to the group.

"Morning," I yawned. "Something the matter? Last time I came down to see people looking outside, it wasn't good."

"A truck," Grayson grunted. "Making its way up to us. Must be one of the locals coming to check on us now that the snow's cleared," Grayson said, peering out again. "I'm going to go talk to him. See what he knows."

"I'm coming with you!" I insisted, jumping up to follow him. I hastily put on my boots, coat, and scarf by the door and rushed outside, careful not to slip on the slick ice.

"Go slow," Grayson directed me, holding up both hands.

"I'm trying," I said, sliding a little.

He reached out and I took his hand. Together we made our way up the long driveway to the street, where the truck was slowly rolling up, crushing over the ice on the pavement. The truck came to a wobbly stop at the front of the driveway and the driver rolled down the window. It was an old man, fully bundled up but clear-eyed.

"Hey man," Grayson greeted him like they were old friends.

"Hey there," the guy replied, waving. "Saw you all shoveling snow up here."

"Yeah, we were trying to clear it out since the snow's lightened up a little," Grayson said. "If we smooth it down we might be able to make it out to the airstrip."

"Are you all the folks who flew in last week?" the local asked.

"Yeah, that's us," I piped up warily. "Why?"

He winced. "Hate to be the guy to tell you, but I've already been down to the airstrip. My son works there, it's just a skeleton crew right now. Most are still out on account of the weather. That strip's not getting cleared for at least a few more days," he told us apologetically.

My heart sank down to my gut.

"What?" I murmured.

"Yeah, I'm sorry. I just figured you guys might want the heads up on the situation down at the airstrip," he said. "Saw you shovelin' and came on down. But now you know."

"Now we know," Grayson said firmly. "Thank you."

"No problem, man. Hang in there," the local said. He rolled up his window and drove off, leaving me in a state of panic as we made our way back up to the front door.

"What the hell are we supposed to do now?" I asked.

"Alaskan weather is unpredictable. And those airstrip workers... they don't get a lot of time off. I'm sure they're enjoying a break. This ain't a city, we move a little slower out here," he reasoned.

Before we got all the way up to the door, I stopped Grayson. I didn't want to discuss this yet in front of the others. We needed to talk about it ourselves.

"We have to figure something out," I said.

"I know," he sighed. "Landon and I have a schedule to keep. It'll hurt our business if we don't get back in time."

"And all of us have planes back to Los Angeles to catch," I groaned.

Grayson put his hands on my shoulders.

"Calm down," he growled, the look in his eyes so kind and gentle I immediately felt my panic start to ebb away. My shoulders relaxed, and I drew in a deep breath.

"Okay. Okay, just let me think for a second. There's got to be a way around this," I said.

"We can do this, Connor. We can work it out somehow. Together," he assured me.

And that was it. The spark. An idea occurred to me that was so outlandish it made me actually laugh out loud. Grayson looked at me like I had lost my mind.

"Are you feeling okay? What's so funny?" he asked dubiously.

A grin spread slowly across my face as my outlandish idea began to grow legs and take shape. Lots of legs. And lots of shapes. I bit my lip and looked up at Grayson.

"I have an idea," I said. "And I think it's a good one."

16

GRAYSON

CONNOR HADN'T WAITED FOR ME WHEN HE ANNOUNCED THAT HE HAD an idea—he had dashed back into the lodge, leaving me staring after him in bewilderment, but I didn't dawdle for long. This wasn't just an inconvenience, it was a real problem, and not just for Connor.

I made my way back up the snowy path to the lodge and pulled my boots off as I headed inside, making a beeline for Landon's room. To my surprise, I didn't see any of the models or photographers in the lounges on the way to the stairs, and I could hear them in the lodge, but I never met any on the rest of the walk. Considering what Connor and I had just learned, I assumed he had called them all back somewhere private for a heart to heart about what was going on.

I didn't envy Connor at that moment, but then again, I wasn't all that happy with my own task. I had to fill Landon in.

"Guessing by the way you looked when you marched back up here," Landon said as I knocked on the open door's frame and stepped inside his suite, "you don't have great news."

"Looks like the good people of Cornerstone don't have to be up in the air anytime soon," I said, nodding with a weary sigh as I stepped into the room and pulled up a chair to sit down and think. "It won't be their top priority, at least. The airstrip isn't clear, and they don't have the manpower to get it done fast enough."

"Damn," Landon grunted, running a hand through his hair and pacing, joining me in trying to think. "How are the guys back home going to handle it?"

"It's not going to be easy on them, but it won't be the end of the world," I said. "Worst case, we'll have to tell a few people their packages are arriving late. Nothing too out of the ordinary."

"So what, we kick back a few more days and wait?" he said.

"I'd rather not," I grunted. "They're under enough pressure right now, so if there's a way we can get our birds back to Anchorage, I want it on the table."

"I got an idea," Landon said, snapping his fingers. "We build this giant slingshot, see—"

I wadded up a piece of napkin on the desk near me and tossed it at his head, and he chuckled as he deflected it and I shook my head.

"Smartass," I said. "What do you think the chances are we could head to the closest bar and offer some of the money from this job to help clear the runway?"

"I mean, chances we can try? Could be worse. Odds that anyone will give us the time of day? Maybe not," he replied bluntly.

I let out a slow breath and nodded, knowing he had a point. "Looks like it'll just be us, then. Here I was hoping the last time I'd have to clear a whole damn strip would be that Christmas you stayed with us."

"Hell of a holiday that was," Landon said with a chuckle, grateful for a little distraction from the daunting task ahead of us.

"Didn't scare you off, either," I added, grinning.

"What can I say?" Landon said, smiling gruffly. "Figured if you and your dad were willing to bust your asses to get it done, it must have been worthwhile."

"Well," I said, looking out the window at the two sets of footprints leading to and from the lodge. "You work hard for things you care about. No lie there."

I felt Landon smiling knowingly at me as I looked out the window, and I was sure he was thinking the same thing I was. My company could handle a little extra pressure if it was absolutely necessary. But I didn't want Connor to have to go through that, not just because it could make him look bad through no fault of his own.

Landon and I tossed a few more ideas back and forth, like getting a ride to the nearest town that didn't get hit by the blizzard, or even just outsourcing the job to another charter company nearby. None of the options we came up with were any more dignifying or feasible, though.

A few moments before I was ready to get up and start asking the others for ideas, Landon and I heard the sounds of a small stampede of footsteps. We exchanged a confused glance, and I pulled the door open in time to see Connor step in front of it, a bright grin on his face, followed by all ten of the models.

And the models themselves didn't look like they were about to head out on a shoot. The ones with longer hair had it tied back out of their eyes, they all wore either their own street clothes layered up or the closest thing they all had to street clothes that they could scrounge up among the bunch of them, by the looks of things. I stared at the group, baffled, and then I realized that all of them looked every bit as enthusiastic as Connor.

"What's all this?" I asked, stepping aside to let Landon see what was going on.

"I filled all the guys in on the situation," Connor explained, "and we have a solution."

"A solution we all agreed to, one hundred percent consensus," Andrew said from near the front of the crowd of models.

"That's right," Niko said with a firm nod and a warm smile.

"Grayson," Connor said, "you were editing those pictures with us. You of all people should know that this week, everything we've done that didn't involve panicking like a bunch of chickens with our heads cut off, is because you were able to step in and take over on day one," Connor said, giving me a respectful nod from one leader to another.

I was speechless.

"You saved our asses—you too," Andrew agreed, nodding to Landon, who raised a mug of coffee in acknowledgment.

"So, that's what we want to do now," Connor said, letting his smile split into a grin. "I've got a team of ten men who are in some of the best physical condition of anyone else in the business, and every one of them wants to roll up his sleeves and hit the snowbanks with you."

"We want to help clear the snow and get us in the air again," Andrew explained.

"If," Connor said, blushing a bit, "that's something that you think we could do, of course. This could be all one big bust for a reason I don't know about. Which would be embarrassing. But the point is, we're here, we're ready to work, and we want to return the favor you did us by making this shoot stay intact."

I couldn't believe what I was hearing. Part of me had hoped that we could get some help from *somewhere* but the models of all people? I'd known my share of fair-weather friends—people who would be nice to you in person, but as soon as the time came to get down and dirty with some real work or any kind of struggle, they'd suddenly be gone and never have the time. And of all people, I would have expected a bunch of spoiled models flying up from LA would be the first people to shy away from the snow.

But it would seem that I had judged them all wrong, and I had to admit, my face was burning because of it, even though I was smiling ear to ear.

"I don't know what to say," I grunted, scratching the back of my head.

"You could tell us whether you think a team of thirteen able-bodied men could do a better job at clearing an airstrip than just three," Connor said with a wink, and I snorted a laugh before scooping him into a warm, tight hug that nearly lifted him off his feet.

A heartwarming "Aww" went around the group of models as Connor pressed a kiss to my lips, and I felt his back pop under the pressure of my hug. We were both laughing by the time I set him back down, and I waved a dismissive hand at the group, still grinning.

"Alright, none of that," I said in a fake-grouchy tone before looking around at the group of people I felt like I might actually be able to call friends. "Good job, you warmed this hardass's heart. You're good men all of you. Now if you want to work side by side with me and my kin, you're all going to need to be able to follow my orders on the snow, and I'm not easy to work for. How does that sound to you?" I asked as if addressing my own little army.

The group cheered almost in unison, and Diego even whooped, breaking my facade and making me snort a laugh as I waded through the sea of models, many of whom patted my shoulder on the way through. I led them down the hall with Connor and Landon falling in step behind me, and my heart was pounding.

We might just have a shot at getting out of here in time.

"Round up as many snow shovels as you can find," I barked to the group as we trudged outside and started heading for the nearest storage shed we could find. "I want everyone with one in hand, and if not, buddy up with someone who does, because you'll be taking rotating shifts. I want all hands on deck, meaning everyone who can physically manage to handle a shovel is right in the thick of it."

We gathered all the supplies we could, and we piled into the same couple of SUVs that got us up here from the airstrip in the first place. All bundled up in the clothes we'd need for the work, the men hardly looked like statues carved from marble anymore. I drove the first car, and Landon took the second as we made our way down into town.

Cornerstone was a quaint little town, even by Alaskan standards. Most small towns like this lived and breathed workers, but this place was a tourist stopover, and the locals knew it. The number of cute cottages with roofs weighed down by snow and cozy bed and breakfasts told me that much.

The airstrip itself was exactly as the local had described it—far from ideal, mostly still caked in snow, and not nearly in working condition. We brought the SUVs to a stop and spilled out. Even though our vehicles were big, we must have looked like clown cars, with over a dozen tall, muscular men pouring onto the snow. I noticed a few locals peeking out of their windows up on the hill above us, and I gave a soft chuckle as I watched the small cloud of my breath plume out in front of me.

"Oh my god," Connor breathed as he looked out on the plane of snow before us.

"Yeah, flat spaces aren't great for keeping the snow off," I growled, recalling all too many memories from my own hometown of battling the elements shoulder to shoulder with other pilots. "So let's not waste any time."

Before turning to the rest of the guys, I stood with Connor at the front of the SUV and smiled down at him, putting both hands on his shoulder. "And listen," I said. "I don't know what you did to convince those guys to do something that sure as hell isn't part of their job, but you get the credit for this one."

"Not happening," he countered with a sly smile. "You're the one who can actually keep people motivated."

"Then we'll settle this after we're done here, how about that?" I asked, and Connor's face broke into a grin before I turned to the models and spoke in a louder voice. "Alright, I want at least one Scandinavian per group, if the rest of you haven't held a shovel before! Connor, Andrew, Niko, and Kristian, you're with me!"

We worked better than I could have hoped. Between me and Landon, we marshaled the models into a capable work crew to start chipping into the snow bit by bit. I gave clear instructions on which areas were the most vital to clear out, and Landon went inside the airstrip (guided by a bewildered office skeleton crew who hadn't been expecting anyone) to inform them what we were doing and see if they had any supplies to help.

Within half an hour, a small crowd of townsfolk had come wandering down to see what was going on. Men clearing snow was a common sight. A troupe of beautiful strangers clearing snow off an airstrip was enough to make local news, apparently. Eventually, I sent Connor across the field to talk to what looked like a two-person reporting team. I didn't know whether the attention was good or bad, but as Connor put it, there was no such thing as bad PR.

By the time he got back, I was impressed to see a few locals approaching to join the effort.

"Room for a few more?" said a woman's hoarse voice as Connor led the locals over to me, looking as surprised as I did.

"If you've got arms, we won't say no," I called back with a grin.

"Good!" she said. "Maybe *this'll* convince the mayor to invest in some damn winter maintenance."

Hours melted away with burning muscles and when it was all done, we stood on an airstrip that I felt confident taking off of in the morning. I could barely believe it. We lined up by the office and patted each other on the back amid congratulations and cheers among the models, and grateful handshakes with the locals. Turns out, none of them liked seeing guests bust their asses any more than we liked having to.

When our SUVs were finally pulling back up to the lodge, we were a mix of exhausted and happy, and our bodies were aching, but we'd gotten it done. In the morning, Landon and I would be able to pile this crew into the plane and get back with time to spare.

"Hey," I said as I stepped out of the driver's seat and led the way to the door. "I don't know if you've all got any shooting to do, but I think we've earned ourselves a reward. How about we put this place's liquor stocks to the test?"

That was one thing I'd never have to convince a big group of young men to get on board with. The exhaustion melted away, and a second wind took the bunch of them as they cheered and piled inside.

Half an hour later, I was standing at the bar, flannel rolled up to my elbows as I clinked a triple shot of whiskey to Connor's rum and leaned against the bar with him. Andrew was standing behind it, having volunteered to serve drinks on the condition that he get the first taste of a rare bottle of scotch we'd found. We were in the lounge near the kitchen, and the fireplace was roaring and warming the whole side of the lodge. The models were sitting either at the table benches, in the comfortable armchairs, or even sitting by the fire and checking out some of the pictures they took.

"Still hard to believe this is work, for you," I said, chuckling. "I see how much goes into it, but moments like this..."

"Work hard, play hard," Connor said wistfully. "That was always my motto, but I guess I got caught up on the work part and kind of let the play part slip away. But hey, that's life, right?"

"Maybe before this week," I said, turning to face him and giving him a lidded gaze. "Hell, I was the same way. Easy not to make time for yourself. But that burns you out. Makes it that much easier for you to snap. And when I saw you a week ago, you were ready to snap."

"Says *you*, of all people," he said, bumping me with his hip before I slipped an arm around him.

"True, I don't mind making you snap like a twig," I said, chuckling darkly and turning to look down at him. "And speaking of, you're looking pretty fragile right about now."

Connor blushed and took another swig of his rum and coke, draining half the glass. "Is that a threat, or an offer?" he teased right back.

My smile slowly spread, and my hand wandered down to his ass to squeeze it. "Upstairs. Let's go."

17

CONNOR

As soon as the door was shut, I turned around just in time to see Grayson barreling into me. With both powerful hands, he pinned me against the wall. I gasped for breath, taken off-guard by his aggression. But I was far from feeling frightened. Oh no. This was exactly what I was here for. I wanted Grayson to use me, abuse my body to get what he wanted out of it. It felt so fucking validating to be confronted with just how desperately this magical, glorious male specimen could want a guy like me. I never imagined I could be so lucky. I had dated off and on for years, sometimes managing to stumble into a brief but rarely satisfying fling or two. They never lasted long. The magic, or the closest thing to it, always ran out way before I got a chance to really get to know someone.

And while I could acknowledge the fact that in the grand scheme of things, Grayson and I had only known each other for such a short time, there was something between us, something more powerful and primal than either one of us could have ever expected. It was explosive. The two of us didn't have to worry about losing the magic— hell, we *were* the magic. And we fed off of one another beautifully. He knew what I needed before I even knew. I knew how to please him instinctively, without having to say a single word. I had never experienced a connection like this before. This was something brand new. Uncharted territory. But as long as I had Grayson as my guide, I would never be lost.

His strong hands pinned my wrists up over my head against the wall and pressed the full, thick length of his powerful body against mine. I rocked into him, loving the deep growl of appreciation that rumbled from his throat.

"God, you're so fucking sexy, you know that?" he purred against my ticklish ear.

Delicious shivers of pleasure rolled down through my body, head to toe. I whimpered as his free hand began to roam down my frame, groping as it went. He smoothed his hands down my shoulders, my forearms, underneath to the tickly sides of my torso. His fingers traced along every rib, every sharp line and curve of my captive body. I didn't dare move or speak. I hardly dared to even breathe. I didn't want to do anything that might stop him from touching me like this. I longed for that touch, day in and day out. I was fully addicted to Grayson, and I knew it was risky to let my feelings blossom like that, with the future so uncertain. But something in the fire of his gaze or the reverence and possession with which those perfect hands touched every inch of my tensing body kept me coming back for more.

He leaned in and captured my lips in a kiss that started off rather soft and probing, a silent question pressed against my lips. But I answered with a soft moan of agreement, and that was all the encouragement he needed from me. His tongue pushed into my mouth and slid against mine as our lips parted and we devoured one another's mouths with a hungry urgency. He tasted like whiskey, like coffee, like the reflection of sunlight against blinding white snow. He smelled masculine and musky, a prime specimen in a heightened state of desire. Was it some kind of animal magnetism or natural instinct that drove us together? Were we entangled in the world's most beautiful mating dance, both of us wholly committed to pleasing the other in perfect symbiosis?

Even though we were both still fully dressed, it felt absolutely divine to rut up against each other, his cock getting thick and bulging at the front of his pants, sliding hard and long against my own swiftly-thickening cock. My arousal was off the charts. It felt like every cell in my body had been lit by a heavenly fire, burning exclusively for Grayson, for the pleasure I knew he would bring me if I only did what he demanded of me. I was more than willing to follow the rules as long as Grayson was the one establishing and enforcing them.

His hand slid down between his crotch and mine, and I gasped with surprise and delight when he began to tease me, stroking my cock lightly through the fabric of my pants. I sighed and tilted my head back, shutting my eyes as I gave in to his soft, tantalizing ministrations. It felt like heaven come to earth. It felt simultaneously like a dream and like the truest moment I'd ever encountered. Grayson knew precisely how to take control and give me what my sore, tired body needed. He was my drug, but also my doctor. He was the paradise and the ship that would carry me there. He was everything. And I was ready to give him all of me, hands down.

"Keep your hands above your head for me," he growled as he released my wrists.

I nodded and did as I was told, holding my arms up against the wall over my head while Grayson explored my body with both hands. His fingers traced the slope of my neck, the lean muscle of my chest and abdominals. That flame of lust in his eyes only intensified when he slid his hands around to grope my ass.

"You feel so damn good. This— all of this—belongs to me. You understand that?" he growled, his breath hot and ticklish on my neck. Goosebumps pricked up and spread down my entire body as I stood clutched in Grayson's arms. I gave him a breathless nod.

"Yes. I belong to you. I am yours. All of me," I murmured, shivering when he squeezed my taut ass cheeks and pressed his hard cock against my thigh.

I rolled my hips, grinding my shaft alongside his, making us both groan in a symphony of pure pleasure. Grayson grabbed my face with both hands and captured my mouth in a fervent kiss, all slippery tongue and biting teeth. A spiral of white-hot desire ripped through me as I felt his teeth bite down gently on my thick bottom lip. I whimpered and shivered, making him smile at me like a predator advancing on its prey. And when I really thought about it, that might as well have been the truth. He was stronger than me—impossibly well built. He knew how to handle himself as well as me. It was freeing, in a way. I was usually preoccupied with withholding control, but with Grayson, I felt utterly safe giving up the reins. He would never do anything to make me regret it. He only brought pleasure, not pain.

Okay. Maybe a *little* pain, I thought as his fingertips pinched my nipples. But the good kind. The delicious kind of pain that I would end up craving for days after.

So when Grayson stepped back away from me, I couldn't help but look disappointed. He rubbed his hands together slowly, looking me up and down with greedy eyes. He was surveying his territory, what all belonged to him. I was his loyal subject, his toy, his servant.

Whatever he needed me to be.

I just required a little instruction. And luckily, Grayson was all too keen to supply it.

He snapped his finger, giving me a serious look. "Step away from the wall and strip for me, Connor," he snarled. "And do it slowly."

"Yes, sir," I murmured, obediently following direction.

I stepped up from the wall and began to gradually unbutton my shirt, swaying a little as I did so. I was not about to go full-on strip-tease unless, of course, Grayson decided he wanted that. But judging by the impatient desire flickering in his gaze, there wasn't going to be enough time for me to flounce around and get all burlesque up in here. So instead, I just methodically stripped off my shirt and pants, kicking off my shoes and socks until I was standing before my master on nothing but my boxer briefs, my cock straining to burst free. Grayson looked me up and down, licking his lips.

"Tell me what you want," I offered in a low, submissive tone. "Tell me, and it's yours."

"Time to take off those briefs. I want to see that cock of yours," he crooned. I reached for the waistband to pull it down, but he stopped me sharply. I peered up to see a burning light blazing right back at me. He was insistent. He was particular about what he wanted and how.

"No," he commanded. "I want to do it."

So I lifted my hands in surrender and held my breath while Grayson slowly slid my briefs down. My cock, long and stiff, bounced free in the cool air. I groaned as Grayson's hands worked their way back up my legs. He started with massaging my calves, then my thighs, and then he only lightly brushed over my cock on his way to grope my hips. I bit my lip as I looked down at him. It seemed backward to have him kneeling and me standing, but then he promptly stood back up and pointed to the bed.

"Get on that bed. On your back," he ordered.

"Yes, sir," I murmured.

I hurriedly climbed up on the bed and scooted back to rest my head on a pillow, watching the show. Grayson was stripping out of his clothes now too, and I could hardly breathe in anticipation of seeing his massive cock again. As soon as he tugged down his boxers, I inhaled sharply. Even though I had seen and felt and tasted that cock many times before, I was still always amazed at how beautiful and huge it was. He had the perfect cock. Slightly curved upward, thick enough to stretch my cheeks, and long enough to nearly gag me. My mouth watered impatiently for him.

"Tell me what you want, Connor," he growled.

"I want to taste your cock," I replied. "Please."

"Well, since you did ask so nicely," Grayson purred as he crawled up onto the bed.

I held my breath and watched as he moved closer and closer to me, taking his time to ramp up my anticipation. I was a naturally restless, impatient person. I liked to get things done straight off the bat. But I could be patient if I had to be. Especially when I knew how satisfying the pay-off would be. Grayson moved up and spread my legs apart, eyeing my cock as it twitched and twinged with intense need. I felt like I was a rubber band pulled taut, barely restraining the lustful beast deep inside me. But I knew to be patient. To wait. Because Grayson was the only man capable of taming and guiding that beast to the fullest scope of pleasure. I had to be good and behave myself if I wanted that sweet release.

Grayson took my cock in one hand and began to slowly, lightly stroke it up and down. I gasped and tilted my head back, closing my eyes. I rolled my hips and bit my lip, loving the sensation of his thick, calloused fingertips brushing against the silky smooth skin of my cock. He was teasing me, arching me ever higher and higher without bringing me close to the edge. It was driving me crazy, but only in the best way possible. He certainly knew how to build tension, make me crave him even more. I shivered as his fingers circled the sensitive head of my shaft. His other hand slid down to cup my ass, giving it a tight, possessive squeeze.

"Oh yes," I breathed.

"Mm, you like that?" he growled. "You like when I show you who's in charge here?"

I nodded vigorously. "Yes. God, yes."

"You want to taste this big cock, Connor?" he snarled, rearing back on his knees to stroke his own massive cock. It looked so heavy and thick with pent-up tension. I was salivating at the thought of tasting him.

"Yes. Put your cock in my mouth. I want to feel you on my tongue," I murmured.

"Lie back. Open your mouth wide," he commanded.

I followed his instruction, feeling tingly all over with anticipation. He maneuvered himself to straddle my face, sliding his full, thick cock into my mouth while he bent over me, his hands closing around my own shaft. I eagerly tugged his length into my mouth, flicking my tongue around the head and moaning as he pushed deeper and deeper in. My cheeks ached, my eyes watered, and my cock was twitching as he stroked me. It was almost overwhelming—the sensations of my mouth and throat being stuffed full of salty, musky cock and the two calloused hands sliding up and down, swiveling expertly around my own.

Grayson picked up the pace, managing to balance perfectly. He braced himself on one hand while the other jacked me off. All the while, his cock was shoved deep into my mouth, the tip dripping salty, tempting precome down my eager throat. I loved being his submissive, being underneath him in every imaginable way. He made me feel good to give in. He made it easy to let go of the reins and just let someone else be in charge of my pleasure for a while. I moaned around his cock, my hips rocking involuntarily with every swoop and squeeze of his hands around my shaft. It felt so fucking good, and I was quickly careening toward the edge—the brink of no return.

Grayson knew this. "Not yet," he growled. "I'm not finished with you."

I moaned and whimpered as he slid his cock out of my mouth. It took a few moments for me to work my jaw back to a normal position. I knew I was going to have a massive headache or jaw pain later, but it was worth it. God, it was so worth it. I watched with wide eyes as Grayson slid off the bed and walked off toward the en suite bathroom. I sat up in bed, pouting a little.

"Wait! Where are you going?" I asked plaintively.

He gave me a devilish smirk. "I'll be back in just a moment."

I waited impatiently on the bed while he puttered around in the bathroom, then came back out holding a shiny square wrapper and a bottle of lube. Instantly, my body seemed to fire right back up. I bit my lip, my heart racing as I watched him unwrap the condom and seductively roll it over his gigantic cock. It could barely fit, and I was beyond impressed. He then sauntered over to the bed and ordered me to lift my legs with a gesture.

"Open up that sweet little hole for me, Connor," he crooned. "Spread yourself open."

I grabbed my ankles and stretched my legs up as far as I could manage, giving him ample space to do whatever he wanted with me. Thankfully, I was a regular yogi back home, so these flexible positions were somewhat comfortable for me. I shivered with excitement as Grayson squirted lube onto his fingertips. He slowly began to massage the tight band of muscle around my asshole, loosening them up and helping me relax for him.

"Touch yourself for me," Grayson commanded.

I reached down and began to lightly stroke and pump my cock while he slowly slid one finger, then a second, inside my hole. I cried out and bucked against him, overwhelmed with the intensity of the pleasure. He continued to finger my ass until finally, I was getting close. Before I could come, he withdrew his fingers. But I didn't have to wait long for what came next. He lined up the swollen head of his cock at my slick hole and pressed inside with one fluid movement. I cried out and grasped at the bedsheets, holding on for dear life as Grayson bent me over like a pretzel, folding in on myself while his cock speared deeply into me. He brushed against my prostate and I moaned, tears of pleasure burning in my eyes. He began to thrust harder and faster, and it was abundantly clear that both of us were finished wasting time. We just wanted the pay-off, the big explosion.

I clenched my ass as tightly as I could manage and continued stroking myself while he fucked me mercilessly, pounding into me so hard I was seeing stars. Finally, both of us started to seize up, that tingling promise of a climax within reach. Coming closer and closer by the millisecond.

"You ready for me?" Grayson snarled.

"Yes! Give it to me, please!" I choked out.

One moment later, he grabbed my hips with both hands, holding me in place while my cock spurted hot, sticky come all over my taut stomach. At almost precisely the same time, Grayson exploded inside the condom, thrusting a few more quick pumps before pulling out. He curled up beside me, pulling me close to him as we panted, coming down from the supreme high of being together as one. The vibe in the room settled back from frantic to languid, as we lay tangled in bed together, not even caring about the sticky seed drying on my stomach or the condom full of come at the end of his cock. We didn't want to move. Not yet. It was just so delicious lying in bed next to one another. There was a kind of magic between us hanging now in the stillness and the near-silence, only broken up by our rhythmic sighs and gasps. Gradually, we returned to reality, and Grayson kissed the back of my neck, giving me chills.

"Come on," he whispered in my ear. "Let's get cleaned up."

"Okay, fine," I whimpered.

I felt him slide away from me, leaving my back cold and exposed.

His hand pulled at mine and helped me out of bed. I was stiff from intense lovemaking, but it felt good to follow him across the room to the en suite. We stepped inside, and he turned on the shower. As the bathroom slowly filled with deliciously warm steam, we climbed into the shower together, letting the hot spray wash away the filth and grime on our bodies. The water soothed my sore muscles and I took my time washing my hair and body while Grayson watched. I began to feel a little self-conscious under his gaze.

"What are you looking at?" I asked warily.

He tilted his head to one side. "You. What else?"

"But why me?" I pushed, realizing this was more than just a momentary thought. It was an insecurity, buried so deep down for years, that was finally surfacing now that I had someone I felt comfortable enough to share with.

"What do you mean, Connor?" he pressed.

I sighed. "I know what I look like compared to those models running around the place. Don't get me wrong—I know I'm objectively a decent-looking guy. But I just have to wonder: in a situation where you could have chosen any one of them, why me?" I asked.

Grayson stepped closer to stand in the hot water with me, cupping my face. He peered deeply into my eyes and I felt so small, so safe in his arms.

"Connor, there is no comparison in my mind. You are exactly what I want. I like you just the way you are, and I'm going to take full advantage of it," he informed me firmly.

My heart skipped a beat. I had not felt this kind of warmth and reassurance in a long, long time. It was still hard for me to see what he saw in me, but his words rang true. I couldn't help but believe he was telling me the truth. He had no reason, no motive to lie. Even though I was his submissive, he still honored my feelings and assured me of my own power, my own charms. I felt validated and acknowledged, but even beyond that, I felt… appreciated. Finally. On a soul-to-soul level.

"You know, I've never felt so at home with someone before," I admitted.

Grayson smiled gently, stroking my cheek with his fingers. "I feel the same way."

"I can't help it. I just want to spend all my time with you," I said. "Is that bad?"

He chuckled. "If that's bad, then I don't plan on being good. In fact, I have a question for you, Connor. Feel free to answer however you see fit," he said cryptically.

My stomach was twisting into knots as I waited to hear his question.

"Go on," I urged him, a little breathless. What did he have in store for me?

"There's this wedding I am supposed to attend. One of my fellow pilots is getting married, and I need a plus one. What do you think? Will you be my date?" he asked.

I grinned, feeling so giddy and light I might just float away. I nodded and stood on my tiptoes to kiss him. When I pulled back, I said excitedly, "Hell yeah! I'd love to!"

18

GRAYSON

I FOLDED THE LAST OF MY CLOTHES IN CONNOR'S SUITE AS HE ZIPPED past me on what must have been his hundredth trip between the bathroom and the closet, and I fought off a smirk. I had always thought that having someone around with the kind of energy Connor had would have been annoying but watching him dart around getting ready for the big interview today was endearing in its own way.

"You need to slow down," I said in my calming, rumbling tone. "You won't do yourself any favors taking it too quickly."

"I'll worry about slowing down when this interview is over," he said with a mild laugh, but I knew that tone in his voice.

He was more worried than he was letting on. Maybe it was just because I could read Connor better than most people, but I had a good nose for when that was happening. I turned around and sat down on the bed, folding my hands calmly between my legs and watched him. He was hurrying around in his underwear and a tank top, which was giving me more than enough thigh and bicep to keep me entertained, but in his hands he held up a couple of sharp-looking bow ties, one of them black and one of them a dark purple.

"Which do you think?" he asked, raising and lowering each had.

"The black goes better with the boxers-and-tank-top look," I teased, giving him a gruff smile as he rolled his eyes. "But for this? Purple."

"That's what I was leaning toward," he said as he set the ties aside and hurried to the bathroom.

I slowly stood up and followed after him, stretching my arms and feeling more relaxed than I had in ages. Maybe Connor had somehow absorbed whatever anxiety I might have had leftover because the guy's thoughts were obviously racing.

Following him into the bathroom, I found him with a pair of tweezers carefully manicuring his eyebrows, and I crossed my arms and leaned against the doorframe to watch him. After a few silent seconds, his eyes started flitting to me when he realized I was watching him.

"What's the matter?" he asked, a smile crossing his face.

"Just watching you overthink this interview," I said simply, and Connor blushed faintly.

"I know, I know," he said.

"We just got over one big hurdle," I said. "We beat Mother Nature, so a journalist like Pete shouldn't be scary to you. Besides, he's on your side, isn't he?"

"Yeah, of course he is," Connor agreed. "It's just the jitters, I'm sure."

"Pretty bad case of the jitters," I pointed out.

"Guilty as charged," he said, smiling at me as he set the tweezers down and looked himself over one more time before running the water and splashing some on his face.

"My point is," I said, stepping behind him so that my body framed his as I watched him, "you shouldn't psych yourself out here. The rest of this week has gone well. You did good. Period."

"True," he admitted. "That's all mostly for the models' sake, though."

"We both know that's not true," I countered.

"This interview is the only part that's all on me, though," Connor said, drying his freshly shaved face with a towel and turning around to look up at me. "Sometimes I joke that I like managing because I do better at handling other people's problems than my own. Then again, that's probably not a very good joke, just a fact."

"Funny to watch you forget that sometimes," I said playfully, reaching over and squeezing his hips before leaning in to kiss him on the lips.

He blushed and smiled warmly, but I was starting to think he could use a little something else to get his mind back in shape, so he could knock this last thing out of the park. It was funny, Connor was the manager of the models, but I'd grown to like my unofficial role as Connor's handler. It suited both of us.

"Then it's a good thing you're around to keep me grounded," he said in a soft tone as I broke the kiss and drew back slowly. "Kind of ironic, since you're a pilot."

"Speaking of," I said, holding his hips against mine and slowly rocking side to side. "You mentioned you were moving up to Anchorage after this, didn't you?"

"I think I remember saying something like that, yeah," he teased with a brighter grin, looking a little relieved that I had been the first to break the ice on that question. "Very soon after this, actually. Of course, if I bomb this interview, it might not happen."

"You are not going to bomb this interview," I said kindly but firmly, giving his hips a warning squeeze. "I don't want to hear any more of that out of you. I don't like it when people don't believe in my man," I added in a lower, huskier tone as I leaned forward.

Connor's cock grew—I felt it swelling against mine, and it made me happy to know that I could have that effect on him even when he was seemingly distracted by everything around him. I wanted to be his distraction. I wanted to command his full attention whenever I wanted. And now, I could do just that."

"Well, with your vote of confidence," he said, "then yeah, I might very well be managing a modeling agency of my own up there. Down there, I guess. It's strange to think of Anchorage as further south," he added with a laugh.

"I know this place that's just outside the downtown area," I growled, closing the already small distance between us and putting my arms over his shoulders, giving him a lidded, hungry look. "Nice, down to earth pub, all wood interior, fireplace in the front, beer garden in the back. Lots of shady corners to get lost talking for a few hours."

"Talking doesn't sound like something *you'd* be interested in doing for a few hours with anyone," he said, grinning.

"Maybe not," I admitted. "You'd be the exception, but then again, talking's not all I'd like to do with you at some of my favorite spots around town."

"Like what?" he asked, feigning perfect innocence as he tilted his head to the side and looked up at me with those big eyes that made me lick my lips and melted my heart.

"A little stress relief to keep your head clear for big days like this, for instance," I growled, lowering one of my hands to his stiffness. "A firm hand to remind you who's in charge."

"I'm a little easier to keep on a short leash if I'm close by, I suppose," he teased, squirming his hips against mine and putting his hands on the counter to brace himself against my looming figure. "And I know I *might* have a little more to learn about adjusting to Alaska," he added with a wink.

"You have no idea," I rumbled.

My hand slid up to the back of his head and caressed it before I tugged him back by the hair, exposing his neck. I stroked it with my other hand, admiring how smooth and soft he was to the touch. The thrill of holding Connor and doing whatever I damn well wanted with him was even stronger than it had been the first time I pulled him somewhere private with me, and it wasn't getting dull on my watch.

I kissed his neck, moaning into the scent of his cologne. It was classy, professional, but still rich and masculine in a way that drove my senses wild. I started feeling his broad shoulders and ran my hands down the muscles of his back while his own hands felt my taut ass and groped me. His right hand wormed its way between my thighs, and I felt him stroking my shaft with an almost desperate need to please.

The warmth of his palm woke me up in ways that coffee never could, and I let out a stronger groan before I ran my hands down to Connor's hips and turned him around to guide him toward the shower. I ran the water, but I wasn't about to plunge us in and make Connor have to get ready all over again—I just needed somewhere to clean up when I was done with him.

My hand reached into his underwear and pulled his sack out with the heavy cock that bobbed in the now warm air as my other hand acted like a seatbelt, keeping Connor strapped to me. I handled his balls lovingly, kissing his neck to make him feel safe, controlled, and protected.

Being able to provide that for Connor was more of a rush than I could have ever hoped for, and it made me eager to see what the future held for us.

My hand found its way to his shaft, and I started massaging it gently. It was already thick and showing that it needed relief, but at my touch, it came to full attention.

"Good," I growled. "Your body knows me. It remembers what I can do to it. That's only going to get stronger, the more you let me have my way with you."

"If that's supposed to scare me off, it isn't working," he teased, pushing his ass into my cock and my heart pounded in delighted passion.

I firmed up my grip on his shaft and slid it along the smooth, warm length from the bulging tip to the thick trunk, and I didn't waste time. My pace picked up, and I felt his body growing tighter with every stroke I inflicted on him.

He reached up with one hand to hold my arm for support, and his other went to the wall, his muscles flexing and showing themselves for me in a gorgeous, sculpted display while his body readied itself to offer me what I wanted.

Connor's mouth fell open, and I turned my face, feeling my strong jawline rub against his cheek before I pressed a kiss to it and whispered into his ear.

"Come for me, Connor," I growled. "Give it all up for me. *Now.*"

I felt Connor's knees almost go weak, and with a powerful spurt that surprised even him, he started to come into the shower and lean back against me. I held him up and got even more fierce and relentless with every stroke that shook his whole body and drained him shot after shot. He let out a ragged, hot groan that made my cock throb, and as he poured out the last of himself, I thought about how good it was going to feel to do the same in him later.

I turned the shower off and dragged Connor back, and I picked up a towel to dab the humidity off his head and neck and plant a kiss on his flushed face, and for a few moments, he kissed back wordlessly thanking me in submissive, obedient bliss.

"That should feel better," I growled.

"You know how to give a pep talk," Connor said in a hazy, dreamy voice as he beamed up at me and took a deep breath. "Yes. We can do this."

"*You* can do this," I corrected him squeezing his hands.

"That's actually something I wanted to ask you about," he said, furrowing his eyebrows. "You had a big hand in making this week happen, so… if you wanted to get in on this interview, even just for a quick shout-out, it might be good for your business."

I scratched my chin thoughtfully, then smirked.

"You roped me into the photoshoot," I admitted, "so I don't see what a few lines in an interview would hurt. Maybe leaving out most of what I did behind the scenes," I added with a wink.

When we made our way out of the suites, we were both dressed sharply, by our respective standards. I wore my best flannel, rolled as far up my thick forearms as the sleeves would go, and a good set of denim jeans and boots to go with it. I looked rougher around the edges than Connor, who wore a sharp suit that I could just picture him in a clean, roomy office in LA doing what he did best.

We were meeting Pete in the cafe—which was probably the part of the lodge that I'd be missing more than anything else if I was honest. Coffee was still the one luxury I didn't mind shelling out for, and damned if it didn't make for a good way to get a room full of near-strangers having a good time when it was too early for booze.

The journalist was already getting set up with a cup of fresh espresso sitting on the table before him, and he smiled cordially at both of us as we entered.

"*The big day*," he said in a faux-ominous tone, smiling and immediately putting Connor at ease with a soft laugh. "Morning, you two. Glad we're still good to go this morning. Feeling good?"

"I'd say so," Connor replied cheerfully with a glance back at me. "Pete, I was wondering if you'd mind Grayson getting a word in on the interview. Would that irritate any sponsors?"

"If it does, I'll edit it out," he said, looking me up and down. "I know I haven't been exactly a social butterfly this week, but I've seen you two together a lot, so I'm assuming you're in some kind of business agreement?"

Connor and I looked at each other, and we had to keep ourselves from laughing before Connor pulled up a chair at the table and sat down across from him.

"Not at all, actually," he said, to Pete's mild surprise. "Perfect strangers before getting here, actually."

"Really?" he said, sliding his recording equipment forward and glancing between the two of us. "Sounds like you've got a story to tell. Want to grab a couple more espressos and get started?"

We settled in, and Connor gave Pete the whole story of the week. Last night, he had been planning all the various ways he could have possibly spun the story to keep some of the challenges out of the way, but he had finally decided to lay it all out just as it was—especially since I was at Connor's side. He explained how we got into this situation in the first place, how worried he and the crew had been when they thought the week was going up in flames, and how I had stepped in to take charge and play a big part in turning the disaster around.

Pete got interested in me and my business, and I got to talk a little about my company, our work, and of course, I got to brag on my best friends and co-workers, Caleb and Daniel. I remembered Connor saying Pete had only planned for the interview to last half an hour, but we ate up far more than that as the interview turned into a casual conversation about the week that Pete had largely been a ghost for, and Connor relaxed more and more as we chatted.

By the time Pete said it was time to wrap up, I had almost forgotten that we were in an interview at all.

"And I think that'll do it," Pete said, hitting the stop button and taking a breath. "I've got to say, I had this week written off as busy work. Connor, I don't know what they're paying you down in LA, but it's not enough."

"I don't mind that," Connor said with a soft laugh, looking up at me and squeezing my hand under the table with a blush. "There have been plenty of other perks to this job. Trust me."

19

CONNOR

I WAS STANDING OUTSIDE IN THE BRIGHT ALASKAN SUN, SQUINTING AS the light reflected back off the purely white ground all around me. It was a gorgeous afternoon, the birds singing and twittering in the tall evergreens while the sun illuminated the landscape with glittering light. It was truly magical to behold, and for the umpteenth time, I reminded myself just how lucky I was to get to spend time here. Sure, things had certainly not gone as planned. But then, wasn't that the way life worked? Despite all my best efforts, I was learning that sometimes, the only thing you could do was go with the flow, work with the environment you've been thrust into, and keep things moving by whatever means necessary.

For example, we had all woken up this morning to a conundrum that needed solving. Specifically, the snowfall that was gently covering the property surrounding the lodge once again. As it turned out, the snow was pretty damn persistent. But then again, so were we. Everyone was gathered outside in the sunlight, trying to figure out a game plan. We didn't have a whole lot of time left here in beautiful, picturesque Alaska, and today was a rare good-weather day. We simply could not let it go to waste. And it was that impulse that brought me to where I was now, standing guard as Grayson and I arranged the models back into their handy team. They had all showed just how good they were at working together to complete a goal when they cleared the airstrip. It was funny—I had never seen these guys look so confident and self-assured as they were while doing manual labor. Was it something they would want to do on a regular basis? Hell no. They were still models. It was hard enough holding a fitness pose for minutes on end while multiple cameras flashed in your face. They didn't require the added difficulty of, say, shoveling snow every day for months on end.

But they had just enough momentum and camaraderie built up for one more project. There was what looked to be a large storage shed off to the back part of the property, and we were all curious as to what was inside. So all the models were bundled up in comfortable, warm clothes and lined up at the ready with their shovels.

"Alright, everybody!" I called out, clapping my hands together. "We are here right now to complete a mission. That mission is to clear a path through the snow from the lodge to that big storage shed back there. Got it?"

"Got it," said Sal.

"We're ready!" piped up Erik.

"Remember the techniques I showed you all," Grayson reminded them. "Now, go!"

The models started working immediately. It was both awe-inspiring and kind of comical watching them push back against the elements, shoveling snow like their lives depended on it. They were constantly laughing and egging each other on, turning it into almost a soft kind of competition to see who could shovel the fastest and most effectively. Grayson and I stood back and watched them work. I was amazed at their tenacity, but then, I figured this was a great opportunity for the guys to stretch their legs and do something more active. This week, being snowed in, they had all been considerably less active than they normally were back in their natural environments, so this was kind of exciting for the guys. And it was fun to watch. They managed to make quick work of the snow, tunneling a path from the main lodge building to the shed. Tomas and Milan delivered the final shovels of snow from the shed door. The lock on the door had iced over, but Niko artfully jabbed at it with the sharp edge of his shovel and it shattered perfectly.

"Damn, Niko!" Andrew laughed.

"You're welcome," Niko said, with a fake bow.

Grayson went jogging over to the shed, cutting them off to get in front. It wasn't an ego trip—it was just that he wanted to be the first in line to open the door, just in case there was something dangerous holed up in there. After all, the shed had been totally off-limits for quite some time. Who even knew what was in there now? It could have been turned into a hidey-hole for a bear or something. If there was one thing my time in Alaska had taught me, it was to expect the unexpected. Everything in life was a mystery waiting to be unfolded, and that was what made it so exciting, so worth living.

I rushed over and stood back with the models while Grayson carefully removed the shattered, rusted lock and dropped it into a pile of crunchy snow. The doors basically sagged open, a burst of musty air billowing out. The models covered their faces and wrinkled their noses, but luckily the foul smell dissipated almost instantly. Grayson carefully pulled the doors further open, revealing the interior of the storage shed.

"Oh my god," Diego said.

"Holy shit," said Erik.

"Is that what I think it is?" asked Tomas.

"Snowboards!" Niko gasped excitedly. "And skis! Look, there's all kinds of equipment in here, guys! I bet it's all been untouched for so long..."

"Looks safe enough in here to me," Grayson appraised, turning back to look at us.

"Well, boys," I said with a grin, "looks like we found the toys."

The models went rushing into the shed in groups of three, as it was too small to allow much more than that, and Grayson came out to stand next to me. I leaned against him adoringly while the models sifted through the piles of high-quality, mint-condition sports gear. There were, indeed, skis and snowboards and sleds and all sorts of fun equipment for a great snow day. The guys picked out what they wanted and eagerly darted out toward the small slopes nearby. I watched them laughing and chatting, goading one another and messing around almost like kids in a schoolyard. It was clear that they had all needed this break. It was much-deserved.

"Looks like they're having fun," Grayson said, hands on his hips.

I linked my arm with his and rested my head on his shoulder, looking up at him.

"Yeah, they are. I'm almost jealous," I said suggestively.

Grayson arched an eyebrow, looking down at me with those eyes all ablaze.

"Well, we can't have that now, can we?" he growled.

Again, he regarded me with those predatory eyes and I immediately acquiesced right into whatever he wanted of me. Whatever he had in mind for me. Our time together here at the lodge was winding down to nearly nothing left, and I could tell both of us were thrumming with the desire to make the most of the time we had left. We wanted to go out with a bang.

Hard. Fast. And right the hell now.

"Come with me," Grayson commanded. I was helpless to do anything but follow.

We left the winter wonderland scene playing out in the snow and walked back inside. I sighed as the rush of warmth washed over my body, but before I could say a word about it, Grayson grabbed me around the waist and hoisted me up. He swung me around once before carting me off to the bedroom upstairs. I was so giddy and surprised by the romantic gesture that I could hardly stop giggling. That is—until we reached the bedroom and Grayson shut the door behind us, signaling that it was time to get down to business. He pinned me against the wall, combing his fingers through my short hair as he kissed me. His tongue pressed into my mouth, his leg wedging between my thighs. I could feel his cock thickening and going stiff between us, pressing long and hard into my thigh. We rocked against one another, moaning and groaning with pleasure. He swallowed down my whimpers and I eagerly arched my back to meet every roll of his hips. We were grinding together, sliding up and down, getting more and more turned on by the second.

It wasn't long before Grayson was tearing off my sweater, my undershirt, my scarf—he just tossed them all across the room. Goosebumps prickled up on my bare skin as it met with the cool air, and Grayson quickly began to kiss his way down my neck, leaving little kisses along the way. I shivered and smiled, biting my bottom lip as he made his way down. He kissed my collarbone, his hands roving up and down my torso, feeling me up. He tweaked my nipples and I twinged uncontrollably, which only turned him on more. He let out a low, mischievous chuckle and I knew I was really in for a good time.

"You like my hands on your body, don't you?" he snarled against my ear.

"More than anything," I breathed.

His hands smoothed along my biceps and down my forearms to press against my palms. He interlaced his fingers with mine against the wall while he rutted into me, groaning and nipping at the soft, ticklish flesh of my neck just below my ear.

"You deserve this, Connor. You deserve to be claimed," he hissed.

"Yes. Claim me, Grayson. I'm yours," I murmured back, overwhelmed with the way he was pressing up into me.

I could feel every glorious inch of his cock against my taut thigh and I wanted to touch it, to taste it, to feel it stuffing me full. I licked my lips while Grayson's tongue flicked over my left nipple, his hands still holding mine out on either side of my face. His hands moved down to unbutton and unzip my pants, pulling them down as I sloppily kicked off my shoes. He pulled down my pants and briefs until my cock sprang free in the brisk air, stiff and bouncing.

I stepped out of my clothes on the floor and was surprised when Grayson scooped me up into his powerful arms once again. It was another reminder of just how strong he was, just how easily he could bend me to his will. Luckily for both of us, I wanted precisely the same thing he wanted, and he was more than willing to give it to me. He carried me to the bed and cradled me back before stripping off his clothes hastily and getting in bed next to me. Without having to utter a single word, I knew what was to come next.

He leaned back against the headboard, legs apart. His rippling muscles entranced my eyes as I slid over, got on my knees, and bent down to pull his engorged shaft between my soft lips. My warm, wet mouth welcomed his salty precome and his stiffness, and I moaned with appreciation as I began to bob up and down. Grayson rolled his eyes back in his head and reached to press his hands at the back of my head. He pushed down, gently but firmly urging me to take more and more of him down my throat. I swallowed his precome hungrily, letting the smooth head of his cock brush against the back of my throat, nearly gagging me, but I couldn't get enough of it. He rocked his hips, pistoning his cock up into my mouth again and again as I moaned and tried my best to keep up. But soon I could tell he was getting close, and he was nowhere near done with me and my body yet. He pushed me back and snapped his fingers.

"Lie on your back," he ordered.

I immediately moved to flop my head back on a pillow, looking up at him expectantly. Grayson straddled me, grabbing a condom wrapper from the nightstand drawer along with a small travel bottle of lube. I bit my lip, waiting impatiently while he rolled on the condom. He squirted lubricant onto his fingers and rubbed slow, massaging circles around the tight band of muscle around my asshole. I whimpered with pleasure, bucking up into his touch longingly.

"You're so eager for it," he snarled. "Such a hungry little slut."

"Please. I want you to fuck me," I whispered.

He gave me a smirk that was hotter than anything I'd ever seen in my life.

"Oh, trust me. I will," he purred.

He held his cock in position, rubbing the smooth head all around my asshole, teasing me, opening me up for him. I wanted to touch myself so badly, but I knew to wait until he said so. He must have caught onto my desire pretty quickly because that was his next command.

"Touch yourself. Stroke your cock for me, Connor," Grayson ordered.

Somewhat relieved, I began to jack myself off slowly, gradually. I was keeping rhythm with the pace of Grayson's cock rubbing around my hole until he finally started to push inside of me. I writhed and groaned with mingled pain and pleasure, overwhelmed by how amazing it felt. Every time with Grayson was like the first time—new, shiny, intense, unexpected. And yet at the same time, we were learning so much about each other. What made him tick. What made me moan. We were memorizing one another's pathways to climax, and it felt amazing to be doing that with a gorgeous hero of a man like Grayson. I could hardly believe my good luck.

And when he pulled out two lengths of what looked like rappelling cord from the nightstand, I nearly came instantly. He lifted my hands to the wooden poles on either end of the headboard. Methodically, he bound each wrist to the poles, keeping me stuck in position. I watched closely, longingly, as he sheathed himself entirely inside me. I cried out, my vision swimming with the intensity of stimulation. He began to fuck me harder and faster, his hands sliding up and down my thighs while he slammed his cock into my ass. With every stroke, the head of his cock rammed against my over-sensitized prostate. I cried out, arching higher and higher, closer and closer to the edge.

He leaned down over me and tilted my head to one side, freeing up space on my neck. He bit and nipped at my soft flesh while he pounded my ass, my own cock twitching and twanging between our body heat. I clenched and sighed with every thrust, loving the way he marked up my flesh with bruising kisses. I was so excited to look at them in the mirror later and remember just how fucking blazing hot this was, how amazing Grayson was.

"Come for me, Connor. I want to feel you come all over that pretty stomach," he growled.

"Oh… I'm so close," I murmured, losing control.

My hands clenched and unclenched in their restraints as my body careened toward climax. Grayson picked up the pace, fucking me erratically now as he gave in to his own fierce, unstoppable needs. He fucked me hard and fast, just how I wanted it, and then we came together in one massive, explosive moment of heightened sensation. I felt my cock spurt sticky, salty come all over my abs while his cock filled the condom inside my ass. He pummeled into me a few more times and then it was over. We were spent. He collapsed beside me and turned me toward him, reaching up to unbind my wrists. He kissed them where the cords had rubbed my skin slightly raw, which made me feel so cared for and adored as we came down from the shared high of orgasm.

He gazed into my eyes while his hand stroked the side of my face. He looked downright radiant in the diffused white light of the sunny snow day, his face flushed from vigorous sex. I had never seen anything or anyone so beautiful in my life. I was nearly speechless.

But luckily, he wasn't.

"I have to tell you something," he murmured roughly.

My heart skipped a beat. "Okay. What is it?" I asked, a little afraid.

He smiled and stroked my face. "Don't worry. I think it's a good thing."

"Well, come on. I'm on pins and needles here," I chuckled.

"I'm falling in love with you, Connor," he said, plain as day. "In fact, I think I may have already fallen. I love you. I know it, just like I know how fresh snow smells, how a wolf howl sounds. I know it with everything in me. And I think it's high time that I told you that."

I was stunned, happy tears prickling in my eyes. He dabbed them away with the heel of his hand and I laughed, shaking my head at how emotional I was.

"You don't have to say it back," he assured me, but I held a finger to his lips.

"Yes, I do," I murmured. "I do have to say it back. Because it's true. Grayson, I'm falling for you, too. I love you."

A grin spread slowly across his gorgeous features. He dove in to kiss me hard, then laughed gently. "Well, then. I think you might have just earned yourself a flight home in the VIP section, hmm?" he teased.

20

GRAYSON

THE BURNING ORB OF THE SUN IN THE SKY LOOKED JUST AS GOOD AS IT had the day we flew out from the lodge and the town of Cornerstone several months ago. It glistened pristinely above the looming colossus of the mountain Denali, the very same one we'd been snowed in under. And every day since then had made me love the mountain even more.

And at that particular moment, I was hoping it loved me back, because otherwise, this landing was going to be difficult.

"And you are *positive* you've done this exact same thing before?" Connor asked with a nervous edge to his voice as I brought the plane in for landing… with no airstrip in sight. The snowy surface dotted with human figures we were flying toward was as flat and smooth as the last few times I had landed on it, but that hadn't done much to improve Connor's worries about landing on top of a glacier.

And to be fair, those were some reasonable worries. But we weren't always reasonable people up in the Alaskan bush.

Daniel and his groom Wes were getting married right on top of a glacier on Denali, something that a few brave couples had done in the past. But not many of those couples had been men, and even fewer of those couples had flown their *own* planes up for the small, quiet ceremony the guys had planned. That made today feel pretty great.

And it had made Daniel even more proud to get that subtle but noticeable rainbow flag painted on the side of his plane.

"Come to think of it," I teased as I brought us in, getting ready for landing with a cruel grin on my face, "it might not have been *this* glacier I landed on last time. This one looks a lot more unstable. Ah well, I'm sure we'll be alright."

"Grayson."

I gave a hearty laugh as I brought us down, and Connor took a deep breath as the field of white hurdled toward us. But I was only teasing—the landing gear on the plane was specifically made for things like this, and I knew exactly what I was doing. We felt the bump of the touchdown, and the other people already down on the glacier's surface clapped and cheered for us as my plane slid down the indentation that passed for a bush airstrip up on this mountain.

We came to a smooth stop, and Connor took my hand, letting out a long breath before laughing, and wiping a hand over his face.

"See?" I said, standing up with a chuckle. "No big deal."

"I'm going to start keeping track of every time you say that," he said playfully. "And just you watch, I will *not* hold back on the I-told-you-so!"

Minutes later, I was letting my plane's passengers out of the cabin, where most of them looked degrees more relaxed than the non-Alaskans present.

We were all here for Daniel's wedding, and I had just flown in most of the guest list that wasn't already here.

"There he is!" Daniel cried, hurrying across the snow to Connor and me before we embraced each other like the old friends we were. "God, I wish I could have been in the cockpit to see that landing. Don't tell me you practiced."

"Totally did," I lied, laughing and clapping him on the back. "Congratulations, man."

"No, no, no, no," Daniel said with a bright smile, "we're pretending this isn't a wedding, remember? If I let myself think that, I'm going to get all misty eyed and freeze my tears."

"Couldn't have asked for a better day," Connor agreed, shaking Daniel's hand firmly.

"Come on," Daniel said with a grin he must have been wearing all day. "Everyone's here now—let's grab Caleb and figure out where he wants everyone!"

Daniel gestured for us to follow him to the other group that had been waiting for my plane to arrive—Daniel's plane was already landed and moved safely out of the way—and Connor chuckled up to me.

"At least there's no question he's excited," he whispered.

"Daniel always used to say he hated drawn-out weddings," I said, shaking my head. "And he puts on a tough face, but he's nervous as hell inside. It's adorable."

I hadn't been to many weddings, and this was the first one I'd been to that required boots as part of the dress code. We trudged after Daniel, and as we got closer, we got a better look at the setup he had for a truly Alaskan wedding.

There was an arch that Wes had built himself standing proudly in the snow, with ivy and forget-me-nots adorning as much of it as they had room to spare. It was a gorgeous monument of green and purple on a sea of white, surrounded by jagged peaks and rock on almost all sides. There were chairs set up on two sides, one for Daniel and one for Wes, but both of them had intentionally short guest lists. We didn't want to crowd the mountain, so to speak, and Wes liked keeping things simple.

Naturally, the group we made a beeline for was our closest friends and family.

Caleb stepped forward to greet me with a warm hug when we reached them, and Elliott did the same close behind him while the others shook hands with Connor. Heather stood among us, looking radiant and almost more emotional than even Daniel—or Wes's parents, who were on the other groom's side of the wedding with him hugging their son and letting happy tears flow.

"Can you believe it?" Heather said, nodding over to them. "I don't think I've seen his whole family before, but who knew a bunch of giants could cry like that?"

"You haven't seen anything, trust me," Daniel said with a laugh, shaking his head and looking around at everyone. "And speaking of..."

"Don't," Caleb warned with a teasing grin.

"You guys—" Daniel started, eyes panning all of us as he started to get misty-eyed.

"Don't," I joined in, grinning but unable to stop myself from letting my emotions get the better of me.

"—are the best family I ever could have hoped for," he finished, smiling warmly at all of us, including Elliott and Connor, who were both part of the family, as far as all of us were concerned. "Thanks for coming up here with us."

"If you think we'd miss this for the world, you're kidding yourself," I said.

"Yeah," said Elliott, crossing his arms. "And believe me, if we didn't like you, I would not have volunteered to get in a plane bound for the top of a mountain."

The pilots among us laughed, and soon, we noticed Wes waving for our attention and all looked to each other.

"Alright," Daniel said with a smile. "Everyone remember everything from the rehearsal? Good, me neither. Let's go get ready."

Half an hour later, the guests were seated, and their heads turned as music started playing. Everyone who was in the wedding stood in the cabin of Daniel's plane, lined up side by side, and in a charming break of tradition, there was no groom waiting at the arches—not yet, anyway.

Heather and a man Wes had introduced to me as Emmett—one of his fellow firemen—were the first to make their way down the stairs, into the snow, and down the aisle to take their places in the wedding. Tears were rolling down Heather's eyes already, and as much as I had tried to avoid it, I was feeling emotional as well. Having everyone together in one place was making me think of how much everything had changed since we started bringing our men home with us, and when I stood back, it painted a beautiful picture.

Caleb and Elliott came down next. Elliott had the dignity of getting to add the title Professor to his name thanks to a stunning, tenure-track position he landed at the University of Alaska-Anchorage and his groundbreaking work that started with a remote little research station off the west coast of the state. Caleb, who was responsible for a huge series of contracts we had gotten with the university, attended lectures with him every so often to keep a room full of rowdy freshmen "intimidated." Caleb had grown from the gruff kid I made friends with so many years ago to a man who smiled more often than not, and it made me a damn proud friend to see that gleaming engagement ring on Elliott's finger. They were planning their own wedding on the island where they met, but it was planned a long ways off to give Daniel some space.

It was our turn next, and I looked to Connor before giving his hand a light squeeze and nodding. We started our march down the "aisle," and the scene couldn't have been warmer in person.

Connor's career had simply skyrocketed after we got back from the lodge. The project that the whole team had worked so hard on took off, and in fact, the whole story got some news attention thanks to the locals who helped us out with the snow clearing efforts. Connor got his promotion, and his office was in the nicest part of downtown Anchorage with a stunning view of the city, and he brought a steady stream of business. I had flown him in personally, and I even saved him the trouble of finding a place to live—we hadn't spent a single night apart since he moved up here.

And it wasn't just his career that week helped.

The shout-out we got in the interview during the week at the lodge got the attention of a few companies who'd started thinking more seriously about setting up connections in the photography world in Anchorage. That meant a huge boom in business for us—so huge, in fact, that we all realized we had the resources to open a second airport. The only question was where to put it, because we already had a manager lined up: Landon had been glad for the chance to spread his wings on his own, and it just so happened that Andrew, the American model we'd gotten to know at the lodge, decided it was time for a career change, and he just so happened to have an expired pilot's license that wouldn't be any trouble to renew.

We walked down the aisle and saw Daniel's immediate family on one side, shivering but looking delighted and supportive, and Wes's family on the other, all large and as gruff-looking as the man himself. One by one, we lined up on either side of the aisle. I stood on Daniel's side, closest to where he'd be arriving. As the best man, it was my place.

When the grooms descended the plane and the music changed, I heard Elliott fight back a sob down the line as the two approached. I glanced over to Connor, who beamed at me—probably thinking of the proposal I was saving up for him later this year.

I could barely pay attention to everything the minister was saying. I made eye contact with each and every one of the guests—even David and Chuck, who were standing by for pictures and looking just as choked up as everyone else. By the time I snapped out of it, I realized that the vows were being exchanged, and my heart did a somersault.

"I do," Wes was saying, beaming down at Daniel with pure love in his eyes.

"And do you, Daniel," the minister asked, "take Weston to be your lawfully wedded husband, to have and to hold, in sickness and in health, in good times and woe, for richer or poorer, keeping yourself solely unto him for as long as you both shall live?"

"I do," breathed Daniel, barely able to get the words out—his eyes were gleaming with tears.

"Then by the authority vested in me by the state of Alaska, I hereby pronounce you husbands, Mr. and Mr. Glover. Weston, you may now kiss your groom."

The applause that rang through the icy mountains warmed our hearts, and I felt a hot tear roll down my cheek as I watched two of my best friends embrace, thinking about how lucky each one of us had gotten.

In a daze, minutes later, we hurried to Daniel's plane, where David had us all lining up for a group photo. Caleb and I stood on either side of Wes, and all our men stood in front of us. We were pilots, men whose hearts were supposed to be unbound and free as the winter winds. But the one thing I'd found true about life up here is that it was never predictable, and sometimes, that meant very, very good things.

I slipped my arms around Connor, and all of us leaned into each other with broad grins as David got ready for the picture.

The camera flashed, and forever saved the first day of a bright future.

THE END

ALSO BY JASON COLLINS

Submission Series

Obedience (Submission Book 1)

Once Burned (Submission Book 2)

Defiance (Submission Book 3)

Worth the Weight Series:

Weight for Love (Worth the Weight Book 1)

Hard Tackle (Worth the Weight Book 2)

The Bodyguard (Worth the Weight Book 3)

Standalone Novels:

His Submissive

Protecting the Billionaire

The Weight is Over

The Boyfriend Contract

Chasing Heat

Dom

Weight for Happiness

Straight by Day

Raising Rachel

The Warehouse

The Jewel of Colorado

Love & Lust